A MATTER OF CLUES

A MATTER OF CLUES

by

MONICA MARSDEN

A light-hearted Rhodesian Adventure
for Girls

THE CHILDREN'S PRESS
LONDON AND GLASGOW

For
G.M.
whose powers of persuasion
were such that this book was
finally written.
With love.

CONTENTS

CHAPTER I

"THANK GOODNESS, that's the end of school," said Julie Kennedy, with a sigh of relief.

"Three lovely weeks of holidays," agreed June, her twin sister, as she threw her attaché-case into the corner.

It promptly burst open and an astonishing variety of books, pens, pencils, rulers, geometry instruments, gym shoes (always known as tackies in Rhodesia), and a shower of paper was at once strewn across the floor.

"D-d-darn it," exclaimed June, with admirable presence of mind, as she saw her mother coming into the sitting-room.

"Evidently you two have broken up," said Mrs. Kennedy, with a smile.

"Darling, it's wonderful," exclaimed the twins, flinging their arms round their mother in an access of affection.

"Just think—no more having to get up at half-past six," declared June.

"No more breakfast at seven," agreed Julie.

"The day you ever sit down to breakfast at seven will be quite a day," said Mrs. Kennedy. "It's usually half-past, and then you have to gulp it down and try and fasten your shoes, remember your books and yell for

13

Julius to blow up your back tyre all at the same time."

"More than our lives are worth to be late for prayers at ten to eight," explained June.

"Can we go and get out of this revolting uniform, Mother?" asked Julie.

"They are *not* revolting," protested Mrs. Kennedy, looking at her two daughters, identical in their charming, pleated grey dresses, collared and belted in scarlet, with short scarlet jackets over them, and wide-brimmed grey felt hats encircled with the ribbon and badge of the school.

"They may not be to most people, but they're hideous on us," explained June. "Why, oh why, did you have to send us to a school that had scarlet as one of its colours? People shudder every time they see us."

"More to the point is, why, oh why, did you have to let us be born with flaming red hair," laughed Julie. "It certainly does scream with the school red."

"Never mind, darlings, it's not as bad as that," said their mother. "Anyway, off you go and get out of those frocks, if you want to. Leave them in the clothes basket, and they can be washed and put away."

Ignoring the burst school-case in the corner, the twins shot out of the room and down the passage to their own big bedroom, the windows of which looked out on to the big lawn bounded by the bougainvillæa hedge, now in full bloom.

The Kennedy twins were nearly sixteen, and the despair of their friends and their school mistresses.

Only their mother could tell the difference between them, although Mr. Kennedy always insisted that he could sort them out. In actual fact, although the twins would never have admitted it, only they themselves knew which was which, for Mrs. Kennedy had been known to address Julie as June. Not that June or Julie had corrected her.

In school uniform they could never be distinguished one from another and, since they were both in the same class, with about the same school marks, since even their handwriting was deliberately similar, and since with a very pronounced sense of humour they often deliberately answered to each other's names, nobody found life really dull anywhere near them.

In fact, more than one form-mistress had been known to moan gently at the news that the Kennedy twins were moving into her form.

They themselves knew that June was the better swimmer, that Julie was well ahead at maths, and that June beat her at languages, including French and Afrikaans which they were both taking. However, it made little difference, for they always swam level in school events and had both won in the Mashonaland Junior swimming championships, and both hoped to swim for Rhodesia some day. They were both quite deliberately equal at examination subjects.

Out of school, they had both learned to drive their father's car and they both went to dances and the popular Rhodesian entertainment of braivleis—similar to the American barbecue party—while they had lately taken up fencing with enthusiasm.

"Hey, come on," said Julie. "Let's go out on to the stoep. Mother'll be having elevenses there."

"Sorry," said June, who had been day-dreaming out of the window. "I'll be with you in a jiffy."

In a few moments, the twins strolled out arm in arm on to the wide stoep that ran the length of the single-story black and white house where they lived.

They were dressed in cool, green, pleated linen shorts with green and white suntops to match, white ankle socks and tackies. Their unruly red curls were brushed and there was no trace of school about them.

As they appeared there was a flurry of almost hysterical barking and two long red bodies, eight short legs and two whippy tails came hurtling at them.

Their two smooth red Dachshunds had suddenly discovered their presence.

"Angel," said June, scooping Sausage up into her arms, where he wriggled and squirmed in a frantic effort to lick her face.

"Beautiful," said Julie, as she stooped down to fondle Mash's silky red ears.

"And after that civic welcome, come and sit down," said their mother from the depths of the long cretonne-covered chair in which she was lying. "Julius is bringing out coffee and buttered scones any moment now."

"Scones?" asked June in surprise.

"Since you didn't fail to inform him this morning that you would be home early, because it was 'azego' school for the next three weeks, he thought he'd bake some for elevenses just to celebrate," explained Mrs. Kennedy.

"Oh, joy, oh Heaven," carolled Julie. "There's

something to be said for having to go to school when you can get this sort of treatment every time you break up."

Her mother's reply was unheard owing to the appearance of Julius, their African houseboy, clad in a spotless white uniform, his black hands with their curious pale palms carrying a loaded tray of coffee cups and saucers, milk and sugar, a large coffee pot, and a plate of the tiny hot buttered scones he cooked so well.

His black face was split in a wide grin that showed his white teeth, the front ones filed to points according to his particular tribal custom.

"Coffee, scones, '*Nkosikaas*," he said politely, and set the tray on a small stool in front of Mrs. Kennedy.

Then he looked at the twins.

"I take books?" he asked, with a slight jerk of his head to the sitting-room.

"Oh, yes, please," said June quickly, before her mother could protest. "Just put them in my room, Julius."

"Yes, Piccanin Missus," he said, and went silently in to the sitting-room, his bare feet making no sound on the polished red concrete of the stoep.

In a few moments, the twins were sitting comfortably in the canvas chairs which, with small tables and a radio, furnished the stoep.

Coffee cups were at their side, and they were steadily eating their way through the piled-up plate of scones, anxiously watched by Sausage and Mash.

The third family animal, an extremely aristocratic

Siamese cat with an unpronounceable Chinese name, but who usually agreed to answer to Chang, was slowly and delicately lapping the saucer of milk near Mrs. Kennedy's chair. Inasmuch as she scarcely belonged to anybody, she might be said to own Mrs. Kennedy.

"Any plans for the holidays, mother?" asked Julie, the worst pangs of hunger satisfied.

"Nothing very much," said her mother. "I suppose you'll be swimming now the baths are open again?"

"Rather. Thank goodness they've decided to open them earlier this year. It was hopeless to keep them closed right through these hols, and only open them in September when the schools go back," agreed June.

"Too cold in June, July and August," said Julie.

"Not always," cut in her sister. "How often have we been out to Mermaid's Pool in August?"

"Oh, yes, but it's been pretty icy," said Mrs. Kennedy.

"Well, Mermaid's is river and much colder than the town baths," explained June.

Mermaid's Pool was a popular weekend resort about twenty-five miles out of Salisbury, and, among other amenities, included a large, natural, tree-fringed pool filled by the small river which poured down the steep, rocky hillside, and overflowed from the pool itself to continue its meandering way.

"I suppose Dad can't take a weekend off," said June thoughtfully.

"Why? Where do you want to go?" asked her mother.

"I thought it'd be rather nice if we could drive over to the Eastern Districts for a long weekend," said

June. "We could go over on Friday, perhaps, and stay at the Vumba or at Inyanga for a couple of nights."

"That'd be lovely," agreed Julie. "Can you persuade him to do that, darling?"

"I might try," smiled Mrs. Kennedy. "Not this weekend, or next, but probably the one after that he'll be able to get away by midday on the Friday."

"Oh, good. That means we could get there Friday night, and perhaps we needn't leave till Monday morning. It'd be lovely to see the mountains again," nodded June.

Salisbury, the Rhodesian capital, lies in the centre of a large, flat plateau, but the Eastern Districts, sometimes called the Highlands of Rhodesia, are a great tourist attraction, and being only a few hours' drive and with several large luxury hotels, are very popular for holidays.

"Father's home to lunch to-day," added Mrs. Kennedy. "You could ask him then and, if he agrees, you'd better telephone Leopard Rock or Rhodes and book some accommodation for us."

The girls nodded and spent the next hour idly discussing the immediate future.

After that, they gave in to the whining pleas of the little dogs and took the two excited Dachshunds for a walk up the tree-lined avenue in which they lived, and round a couple of blocks before returning to their own garden.

Mr. Kennedy appeared at lunch-time, driving his new Vane into the garage before he went into the house.

"Why the garage, Father?" asked Julie, when the twins had greeted him.

"Keep the sun off her," he explained, and the twins laughed.

"You can say that in October, or even in January, and get away with it," said Julie. "But not in August. Let's start again. Why the garage, Father?"

"Keep it out of the way," said her father, pinching her ear. "I'm not using it this afternoon."

"Not using it?" chorused the twins.

"Don't tell me you've taken to walking," added Mrs. Kennedy.

"Not likely. I'm taking the afternoon off," he said with a laugh.

"Well, you've certainly been working very hard just lately," agreed his wife.

"And I look like having to work even harder in the immediate future," said Mr. Kennedy. "Directors from England, for one thing. So I decided to take an afternoon off while I could."

"D'you want to stay at home, or shall we go out?" asked June.

Her father raised an eyebrow in exactly the same way as the twins did when they were surprised.

"Where do you want to go?" he asked, politely. "You notice how well-trained I am," he added, as an afterthought.

"I don't mind," said June. "I just thought it might be nice."

"*What* might be nice?"

"To go somewhere," explained June, carefully.

Mr. Kennedy turned himself round to face his wife. "Where do you want to go, my dear?" he asked.

"I don't know that there are many places," she said. "There's the Aloe Garden at Ewanrigg. There's Mermaid's. But we usually go there at weekends, anyway. What about going out to Zakanaka and having tea there? I believe they give you a very good tea indeed."

"That's the new hotel out on the Bulawayo Road, isn't it, Mother?" asked Julie.

"That's right," said Mrs. Kennedy. "It's about ten miles out. They've got a small swimming-pool, and I believe they're going to floodlight it and have evening dances and goodness knows what else in December and January when the weather's hot."

"It'll rain," said Mr. Kennedy, in depressed tones.

"Only in-between times," protested June. "Anyway, let's go, may we?"

"Certainly," agreed her father. "About three o'clock, then?"

"Lovely," agreed Julie. "May we take Sausage and Mash with us?"

Their father knew better than to protest at the inclusion of the two dogs in any such expedition, and in any case the Dachshunds were very well behaved on all excursions, for they were well accustomed to them.

They always sat up on the back shelf of the car, so that they could see through the back window and were out of the way, and they behaved beautifully when they were out with their family, keeping to heel, and even ignoring the resident cat, should there be one.

"Exactly where is this place?" asked Mr. Kennedy.

"Straight out on the main road, and then a turning to the left which is well sign-posted, and about a mile up a dirt road. Quite a good road, though," said Mrs. Kennedy.

"Oh, I think I know the place," nodded Mr. Kennedy. "Isn't it close to that enormous house of Sir John Wilson's?"

"You mean the place where they had that big jewel robbery the other day?" asked June, and her father nodded.

"They've never caught the thief, have they?" asked Julie.

"Not yet," said her father. "But there's a good deal of fuss about it. People writing to the papers to complain that the police are inefficient and all that."

"Have they any idea who he is?" asked June.

"I shouldn't think so," laughed her mother. "They call him Mr. X in the daily paper, but I doubt if they've anything to go on. He certainly got away with a tremendous haul of stuff."

"Now they're saying that he must have had inside help, and that, in any case, the police are useless," added Mr. Kennedy.

"They always say that sort of thing, don't they?" asked June, and her mother nodded.

"The trouble is that a lot of the stuff was family stuff, so Sir John himself is kicking up a bit," added her father. "Of course, it's all insured, but family heirlooms are usually irreplaceable."

"What makes it worse is that Mr. X got in while the family were having some friends to dinner. Nobody heard a thing."

"They were probably at the soup course," murmured Julie.

"Anyway, avoiding the Wilson mansion, we will head for Zakanaka at three p.m. prompt," announced Mr. Kennedy, and the twins nodded.

It was six o'clock before they reached home again, having spent a delightful afternoon. The pool was small, and the water chilly, but the twins spent about twenty minutes in the water, and in any case the home-made waffles and cream that were served with tea made up for any deficiencies in the pool.

The terrace on which they had tea was warm and shady, and altogether everyone was contented.

As they entered the house, the phone rang, and Mrs. Kennedy answered it.

Ten minutes later, she rejoined her family on the stoep.

"What's the matter, mother?" asked June, jumping up.

"Bad news," said her mother. "I've got to go to Bulawayo to-morrow morning. Oh, it's not very serious," she went on, quickly. "More tiresome than serious. Your Aunt Edith has got to go into hospital for a slight operation. Only a small one, but you know what she is about that sort of thing."

"We do indeed," chorused the twins, remembering previous trouble of the same kind.

"Anyway, I've promised to fly down to-morrow morning and stay there for a day or two until she's all right again."

"Darling, how drear for you. Shall we come with you?" asked Julie.

Her mother dropped a light kiss on the red curls.

"Of course not, my pet. I wouldn't dream of it. It's only annoying just now, when you're both at home."

"Don't worry about us, darling," said June. "We can look after ourselves perfectly well for a few days. Really we can."

"I know you can," agreed her mother. "But I hate not being here during your holidays."

"It's only for a few days, and you can always ring us up," said Julie, consolingly.

"I'll drive you out to the airport to-morrow morning," said Mr. Kennedy. "There's sure to be plenty of room on the eight o'clock plane."

The twins groaned.

"Never mind, darling," said June, heroically. "We'll come along to see you off—even if it does mean getting up once more at half-past six!"

There was a seat available, and the twins and their father saw Mrs. Kennedy off on the eight o'clock plane, which would arrive in Bulawayo three-quarters of an hour later.

Then Mr. Kennedy drove his daughters home from the huge new airport, and left them there to have a second breakfast, while he went off to his office, promising to telephone them a little later in the day to see that they were all right.

He had added that he would be quite free after five o'clock, and suggested an early dinner and then a trip to the drive-in cinema, where a particularly amusing film was showing.

It was while they were having breakfast that Julius appeared with the *Tribune*, and laid the daily paper on the table next to Julie.

She glanced at it idly, for a few moments. Then she let out a strangled gurgle of mirth.

June put down her cup and stared at her twin.

"What's so funny?" she said.

"Mr. X," replied Julie. "You know, the burglar."

"Oh, the Wilson burglary," nodded June. "I know. What about him, anyway?"

"Well, apparently, he's got a bit fed up with everybody saying he was helped over that burglary, and so on, and about the police, too."

"People saying the police don't know their job," said June. "Go on."

"So he's written to the *Tribune* and told them that he's going to do a robbery to-night. He's given them a clue as to where it's to be, and says that if the police turn up there, they'll catch him. But he backs himself to diddle them every time."

"He hasn't!" exclaimed June.

"He has. Look—all this column—and front page headlines too," laughed Julie.

"I should think so—what a story!" giggled June.

The two red heads bent together over the front page of the newspaper, and read the story of the daring burglar nicknamed by the reporters Mr. X, who thought himself so clever that he actually gave the police a clue as to his next burglary and dared them to get him.

"But—are they actually going to publish the clue?" asked June.

"Yes. Look, it says here—Mr. X didn't want to send it to the police, because he wanted everybody to know about it. So he's sent it to the *Tribune* instead, and asked them to publish the thing."

"He must be crazy!" exclaimed June.

"He's got an awful nerve," laughed Julie. "Supposing they catch him?"

"Then that'll prove how clever the police are, and everybody, even down to Sir John Wilson himself, will be delighted."

"Where's the clue?"

"Here." Julie put a finger on a few lines printed in heavy black ink right across two columns.

> "*Is it near or is it far?*
> *Would you go by wheel or car?*
> *By land or water, sea or air,*
> *Go to this house, but have a care,*
> *Many heads are round about.*
> *Many walls return a shout.* (*O, what a rail*)."

"Gee, it sounds tricky," exclaimed June.

"I wonder what it means," frowned Julie, as she read it again.

"Sounds absolute nonsense to me."

"But it must mean something—I mean, it must be a clue to somewhere," insisted Julie.

"I don't see why," declared her twin. "The whole thing's probably a terrific hoax."

"Oh, no," protested Julie. "I'm sure Mr. X wouldn't do such a thing. It sounds quite genuine—I mean, the story. The letter he sent to the editor enclosing the clue, and all that."

"The clue sounds like something out of the Jabberwock, if you ask me," giggled June.

Julie read it through carefully once more.

Then she looked up at her sister.

"I say, June—let's try and solve it," she said, her green eyes alight with enthusiasm.

"Whatever for?" asked June, in some amazement.

"Well—we might be able to," said Julie.

"But half Salisbury'll be doing the same thing by now."

"Well, that needn't stop us," said Julie.

"And supposing we do—what then?" asked June.

"I don't know. Let's try and solve it first. It might be fun," giggled Julie.

"All right," laughed June. "I don't mind. We've nothing to do this morning."

"That's right," agreed Julie. "The sun shines bright, the moon's out of sight, and the roads are still up in First Street Come on."

"Pencils and paper, dictionaries and a couple of road maps," said June. "And don't lose that newspaper, whatever you do."

As she went to the desk to collect some scribbling pads and pencils, she glanced round to see Julie standing at the table, slowly reading through the clue again, and she found herself wondering just where the clue, should they be able to solve it, would lead them.

CHAPTER II

RHYMING SLANG

THE TWINS curled up comfortably in deep arm-chairs, each with a Dachshund equally comfortably curled on her knee, and proceeded to study the clue which Julie had cut out of the newspaper columns, and June had copied on to a sheet of paper.

"It's a bit of a stinker, isn't it," said Julie, after a few moments.

"Let's try and break it down a bit," murmured June.

"How?"

"Take it line by line. You know—like the treasure hunt game we play at parties—rhyming clues hidden somewhere and each one leads you to the next if you can solve the rhyme," said June.

"Oh, I know. Like—violets are blue and roses are red, the clue you'll find if on the mat you tread?"

June laughed.

"It doesn't scan and it's far too obvious, but you've got the right idea."

"All right. Following that principle, you can either bicycle or drive to this place, or, if you're a sailor, you take a boat or fly an aeroplane. Where does that get us?"

"I don't know. It sounds as if it's an airport close to the sea where they're holding a motor-car rally with

29

a couple of stunt races for bicycles," suggested June.

"It's got to be in Salisbury," Julie pointed out.

"Then that's out. No sea," said June, solemnly.

"Hey, wait a minute. I've got an idea," exclaimed Julie. "Supposing——"

The remainder of the sentence was drowned in the hysterical barking of the two little dogs who shot off the girls' knees and tore to the door, skidding on the rugs as they did so.

The noise was increased by a good deal of shouting from the garden, and commands to be quiet and come here yelled by the twins, as they scrambled to their feet and rushed out to rescue whoever was being savaged by the watchdogs.

They reached the garden to see a school friend, Mollie Andrews, and her brother Kit, endeavouring to pacify the dogs.

The twins shrieked at Sausage and Mash, who quietened down almost immediately, and everybody could once more make themselves heard.

"I do admire the ' Trespassers Will Be Prosecuted' attitude of your hounds," said Kit, as he propped his bicycle against the fence. "But do you think you could persuade them that we're not actually trespassers in the full sense of the word?"

The twins laughed.

"We'll try," they said.

"And are we now allowed to come in?" asked Mollie, as she put her machine beside her brother's.

"Don't bother to ask," said Kit. "Just look at the treacherous animals."

Sausage and Mash, satisfied now that their mistresses had appeared, were beaming at the visitors, and frolicking round them with every appearance of welcoming them as long-lost friends.

"They just like to make sure, that's all," explained June, as she picked up Sausage.

"That's right," agreed Julie. "Cautious, that's what they are."

"Well, explain to them that they needn't be cautious with us," suggested Kit. "Teach them to read the ' Welcome ' on the mat when we arrive, will you?"

"We'll try," promised Julie. "Come on in and take your weight off your feet."

The four trooped into the house and sat down comfortably, still chattering.

"My dear, we thought we'd come along and find out if you've seen the *Tribune* this morning," explained Mollie.

"The clue?" asked Julie.

"Yes. We're going to try and solve it," went on Mollie, excitedly. "Don't you think it'd be fun? I mean, if we *can*—and then we thought we might go along to wherever it is and see if we can spot Mr. X."

"You'll have a hard job spotting him in the middle of about five thousand worthy citizens of Salisbury," grinned Kit, his dark face alight with amusement.

"Five thousand?" gasped Julie.

"What on earth do you mean, Kit?" asked June.

"Look, darling, we know we're brilliant—and we know you two are almost as brilliant. But do you honestly suppose that we four are the only people who've decided to solve the clue and turn up at the rendezvous the police hope they're having with Mr. X to-night?" he asked.

"How d'you know we've decided to solve it?" asked June.

"Elementary, my dear Watson," said Kit, pointing to the scribbling pads and pencils, the newspaper folded at the story, the copied clue on June's pad and the cutting on Julie's arm-chair.

The twins laughed.

"After that brilliant display, we shall expect you to solve it at once," said Mollie.

"Let's get back to the five thousand," cut in Julie.

"Picture for yourself Salisbury at the moment," said Kit, dramatically. "Offices are opening, boys are dusting desks, bank tellers are unlocking their little cash drawers, shop assistants are arranging their counters. And, everywhere, they have newspapers in one hand and a pencil in the other. Dictionaries are being taken down from shelves, road maps are being produced from car pockets, and the air lines are being telephoned to find out how far you can go by air and sea, land and water, to get you somewhere close to Salisbury."

"I believe he's right, Julie," said June, solemnly.

"I'm always right," retorted Kit.

"That's what I like about Kit—pure modesty," declared Julie.

"Anyway, so everybody in Salisbury's trying to solve the clue," cut in Mollie.

"I don't see that that need stop us," said June.

"Just supposing every business man and every typist and every office worker and every mechanic and artisan is at this moment trying to solve the clue, why shouldn't we solve it, too?"

"You've forgotten the housewives," Kit pointed out. "But never mind. Of course, my dearly beloved 'earers, there's no reason why we shouldn't solve it, only, having done so, you must expect that one or two others will have done so, and have also been struck by the same idea of trying to spot Mr. X."

"Well, we can decide that part of it later," said his sister, briskly. "What we want to know is—how far have you got with solving the clue?"

The twins looked at her and laughed heartily.

"Like that?" she went on. "Well, to be honest with you, we've reached the same stage. To put it vulgarly, it's a stinker, isn't it?"

"Our very words. We haven't spent much time on it, though," said Julie, and explained that they had been to the airport that morning to see their mother off to Bulawayo, and had really only started on the clue after breakfast, a short quarter of an hour or so before the visitors had arrived.

"Well, don't let us stop you," said Kit, kindly. "We can't do a line of it ourselves."

"Let's all try together," suggested June. "Four heads are better than one."

"Where have I heard that before?" murmured Julie, and was promptly crushed by her sister.

Soon the four were gathered round the big table with, at Kit's suggestion, a dictionary, a road map of

A.M.C. C

Salisbury and the surrounding district, and plenty of paper and pencils. Julie refused to produce ice and wet towels, although Kit warned her that they would certainly be needed before the clue was solved.

Half an hour later, Julius appeared with a tray of cool drinks and a plate of biscuits, and the four sat back with sighs of exhaustion.

"You know, we've got absolutely nowhere," said June.

"Oh, I don't know," declared Kit. "We've managed to rule out some places, such as the Eiffel Tower, Buckingham Palace, the Empire State Building and Idlewild."

"Salisbury Airport and Johannesburg Zoo," added Mollie.

"We should arrive at a solution soon, if it's only by a process of elimination," added Kit, with a grin.

"I don't believe it's a clue at all," said Julie, crossly. "I think it's a nonsense rhyme."

"With Mr. X as Edward Lear? Not a hope, Twinnie. I know for a fact that he's dead," said Kit, solemnly.

"Well, then, something like the Jabberwock," suggested June.

"D'you really think it's a hoax?" asked Mollie, her mouth full of biscuit.

"I don't know," said June, frowning thoughtfully.

"I don't believe it," declared Julie. "I think Mr. X has a sense of humour, and nobody with a sense of humour would try and pull a fast one."

"Why a sense of humour?" asked Mollie.

"Well, just read his letter to the *Tribune*. I think he wouldn't have written that without a sense of humour. Fancy giving the police a sporting chance to nab you! I bet he's fun if you know him."

"I don't know him, but you could be right," nodded June.

"I don't know about a sporting chance," murmured Kit. "I think it's about 99 to 1 against the police or anybody else solving the sporting chance, if you put it that way."

"Come on," said June, suddenly. "The police may be beaten, but I don't see why we should be. Let's try again."

Kit groaned, but the girls would allow for no laziness, and soon they were all at it again.

"Look, take it line by line," suggested Mollie.

"We've done that already," chorused the twins.

"And we finished up on the Equator—because it didn't rhyme too well with near or far. Anyway, that was my brilliant sister's idea," Kit pointed out.

"The next line took us to the R.A.C. offices," retorted. Mollie. "By special request of Christopher Andrews."

"That's me," smiled Kit. "The third line was evidently meant to be Cook's Tours, and the fourth line Julie suggested was something to do with an insurance company, but she wasn't sure which."

"The fifth line was the Rhodes Cinema during a popular film, and the last line was the Whispering Gallery at St. Paul's," giggled June.

"And we decided the last line of all was put in to fox us," added Julie.

"Which leaves us exactly where we started unless you wish to do a world tour," finished Kit.

"This is nonsense," said June, when they had finished laughing. "We know it must be around Salisbury, for a beginning."

"Brilliant, Twin dear," said Mollie.

"Quiet. And it's somewhere near Salisbury that you can reach by road. It's got to have water near it, too."

Kit was busily sketching a landscape. There was a small house in the centre of the page, and, in the distance a road came winding up to it, with a cyclist and a motor-car apparently dead-heating.

"The Zambesi," suggested Mollie.

"A dam," said Julie, brilliantly. "It could be a dam."

"A swimming pool, or the Round Pond," said Kit, and added a small circle in front of the little house, in the centre of which a fish leered at the oncoming car.

"Go on, June," said Mollie. "You may be getting somewhere."

"Then I think the next two lines mean that there's a crowd," said June, slowly.

"What about a party?" asked Kit, adding three tiny couples dancing an energetic rock 'n roll.

"What about the shout?" asked Mollie. " I don't understand that bit."

"Perhaps it's an echo," said Julie.

Kit sketched in a tiny elf with a megaphone in one corner of the paper.

"And the afterthought in brackets?" asked Mollie.

Kit looked up.

"I can't draw an afterthought," he said.

" ' O, what a rail '—I give up on that one," said June.

"Cowboy stuff, perhaps. A hitching post," suggested Kit, and a cowboy with outsize chaps on his legs immediately appeared walking into the little house while a sad-looking horse was tethered to a hitching-rail outside.

Kit looked at it thoughtfully.

" That's all very well," said Julie, looking over his shoulder. "But we still don't know where it is."

"Let's see, Kit," said Mollie, from the other side of the table.

Kit quickly drew a compass sign which closely resembled a question mark, added the compass letters and pushed it across the table.

The three girls looked at it and laughed.

"I don't think it's much help," he said.

"I don't know," said Julie, thoughtfully. "I think we can rule out some of the things—like the cowboy, f'r instance, because there aren't any cowboys in Rhodesia."

"On a point of order, they must have them down south on the big ranches, like the Nuanetsi," said Kit. "But I agree that there're none up here. Go on."

He lent over and put a pencil stroke through the cowboy.

"No horse?" he asked.

"No horse," chorused the three girls.

Kit sadly put another stroke through the horse.

" And the rail?" he asked.

"It could be a rail," said Julie, thoughtfully.

Mollie looked round questioningly at her.
"When is a rail not a rail?" asked June.

"When it's a rail," chorused the sisters.

"All right," he said, crossing out the rail. "If you don't like a hitching-rail, have a railway line."

"No," shrieked the three girls, as he started to draw a baby engine.

"What—not even the Coronation Scot?" he asked, pausing to rub out the engine.

"Not even the Trans-Continental express, or a Rhodesia Railways Diesel," said Julie, emphatically.

"Then that leaves us with a house somewhere near water and a road," said Kit, studying his little drawing. "Plenty of people and an echo. Where is it?"

The three girls studied the drawing carefully.

"There're plenty of roads round Salisbury," said Julie, after a moment. "Let's concentrate on water."

"All right," agreed Mollie. "Rivers—Makabusi——"

"Oh, there are dozens of odds and ends of little rivers that meander about," said June. "Think of all the bridges you cross between here and Marandellas, for instance, and that's only one road."

"It needn't be a river," Julie pointed out. "It could be a dam—or a swimming pool—or——"

"If it's a dam, the biggest is Lake McIlwaine," said June.

"Here—wait a minute—I believe you've got something there," said Julie. "McIlwaine—you can get there by car, or by motor-bike—or even bicycle, if you're really energetic. There are plenty of boats on the Lake, too."

"You don't go there by water," protested Mollie. "You're there already."

"No, no, it's some sort of house—so you can go there by water—across the Lake," said Julie, in some excitement.

The others looked up.

"That's right," agreed Kit, and edged the fish out of the way with a small sailing boat, to the immense amusement of the twins.

"Come on," said Mollie. "Keep it up. I'm sure we're getting somewhere."

"McIlwaine," said Julie. "I wonder if it's McIlwaine."

"That's not enough," her sister pointed out. "It's got to be a place, somewhere that Mr. X is going to—going to burgle, remember? He said so in that letter to the *Tribune*."

"That's right," agreed Mollie. "A house near McIlwaine, then. You can get there by water, by road or—I say, what about air?"

"There's a small landing ground near the Lake, remember?" said Kit. "The local flying club use it. I think it's tiny, though."

Idly, he sketched in a tiny plane, with a pilot dropping from it, a parachute like an umbrella over his head.

"Well, that fits in," said Julie.

"Yes, but there are plenty of houses round the Lake," said Mollie. "Bungalows, proper houses, club-houses, all sorts of buildings."

"Mr. X wouldn't bother to burgle a club-house,"

said Mollie. "I shouldn't think he'd even bother with a bungalow. It must be something bigger and better than that."

The four looked at each other a trifle despairingly.

"Let's have a go at the rest of the clue," said Julie, suddenly. "If the first three lines mean McIlwaine, then the last three should mean the house itself."

"Oh, very bright," murmured Kit, and added a whole row of turrets to the little house.

"I think the clue's in the many heads bit," said June, slowly, after a long pause.

"Many heads and many walls," nodded Julie.

"D'you think many walls really means many rooms?" asked Mollie, rather hesitantly.

"Oh, that's brilliant," exclaimed the twins.

"A large house, then," added June. "Lots of rooms—where's a large house near the Lake?"

"We all know the Lake pretty well," said Mollie. "I mean, we've been out there endlessly at weekends, haven't we?"

The twins nodded, for their father had a great friend with a launch on the Lake, and at least twice a month they all drove out for a whole day on a Sunday, Mrs. Kennedy taking an enormous picnic lunch for the whole party.

They would go on board about ten o'clock, and spend the entire day cruising up and down the vast expanse of water, returning to the *Seasprite*'s moorings as the sun was setting.

On many occasions, Mollie and Kit had been with

them, for both youngsters knew Mr. Paterson, owner of the *Seasprite*, quite well.

"A big house," murmured Julie. "A big house near the Lake."

"The only big house I know anywhere near the Lake is the new Rhodes Hotel," said June.

The three looked up at her, startled.

"The hotel," said Kit, softly. "Well, well, well, there's a clever little thing. We never thought of the hotel."

June looked round.

"Why—d'you think it really is the hotel?" she asked.

"Why not?" said Mollie.

"But—but the walls returning a shout—what's that mean?" asked June.

"They've a big dining-room at the hotel where they have dances at weekends," said Kit, quietly. "They often have a big crowd there, I believe. And a big crowd make a lot of noise—music, dancing, singing, shouting—yes?"

"Yes," said the three girls, decisively.

"Lake McIlwaine Hotel," said Julie, softly. "It all fits in, doesn't it?"

"And they have lots of people staying there— probably it'd be worth Mr. X burglaring the place," added Mollie.

"But what about the bit in brackets about the rail?" asked June, after a moment.

There was a long pause.

"I give up," said Mollie. "It could mean anything, or else he put it in just as a sort of red herring."

"Perhaps there's some sort of rail fence round the place," suggested Julie. "I've never been there."

"That's probably it," nodded Kit. "It's sure to be something like that."

The girls nodded and heaved sighs of relief.

"Well, I think we're brilliant," said Julie, frankly.

"What do we do now?" asked June.

"I wish we could go out to McIlwaine to-night and catch him," said Mollie, enviously.

"That's impossible, ducks," grinned Kit. "But I think we might pass it on to the police, just in case their brains aren't as bright as ours."

"We'll get Father to do that, if you like," offered Julie. "He's a pal of the Chief Superintendent, so he could ring him up."

"That's a good idea," said Mollie.

"I wonder how many people in Salisbury have solved it," said Kit.

"Hardly anyone, I should think. It's fearfully difficult—and we're not sure, even now, if we're right," said June.

"Golly, look at the time!" exclaimed Mollie, suddenly catching sight of the small grandmother clock in the corner of the room. "Kit, we must fly. We're going to be frightfully late as it is."

"Come and swim to-morrow," said Julie, as they all got up.

"Can't, I'm afraid," said Kit. "The Parent birds are taking us to Inyanga for a week."

"But we'll let you know just as soon as we get back," added Mollie. "And do ring up the hotel if you've got anything wildly exciting to tell us about Mr. X."

"We will," promised the twins, and waved good-bye, as brother and sister wheeled their bicycles out of the gate and cycled off down the avenue.

Then they turned back to the house, and went to their own room to wash and tidy up for lunch.

Mr. Kennedy appeared a little late for lunch, having been kept on a trunk call from Johannesburg.

The twins told him of their morning's work in solving Mr. X's clue, and Julie added that they thought it might be an idea if he would let the police know.

Mr. Kennedy laughed.

"I saw Sergeant Haines this morning," he said. "He was passing, as I was coming out of the office, just now. He says that they're having to call up the special police to control the crowds that are going out to McIlwaine this evening—apparently half Salisbury's rung up to give them the answer to the clue."

The twins looked a little crestfallen.

" D'you mean to say that everybody's got the Lake?" asked Julie.

"Not everybody—about fifty per cent.," said her father. "The second favourite was Kariba, quickly followed by the swimming baths, Mermaid's, and a battalion of the district swimming pools like Cranborne, Avondale, and so on."

"What on earth are they going to do?" giggled Julie, as she thought of the harassed state of the British South Africa Police force in Salisbury.

Her father turned away and shrugged his shoulders.
"I haven't the faintest idea," he laughed. "But I certainly don't envy them."

After he had kissed them good-bye, and left for his office again, promising to be home early in time for a meal before they went to the Drive-In, the two girls collected books and cushions and went out into the garden to spend a comfortable hour or two under the big shady tree.

It was a favourite spot, for it was cooler than the stoep on a hot day, and Mr. Kennedy had had a stretch of paving put down to make a steady basis for chairs, stools and tables, and had also bought a gaily-coloured swing seat.

In the height of summer, the whole family practically lived out there, having meals on the small white-painted wrought-iron table, and staying out quite late at night under the shaded lamps that had been hung in the tree.

Presently, Julie looked up.

"You know, I don't like ignoring that last line," she said.

June closed her book, keeping one finger in the place.

"Oh, what a rail?" she asked. "I rather agree with you. I'm sure it was put in for some purpose, but I've no idea what it means?"

"Supposing it isn't really McIlwaine at all," said Julie. "I mean, supposing McIlwaine was a sort of red herring, to attract everybody, including the police. And suppose the real clue was in that line."

June thought for a moment before nodding agreement.

"Could be," she said, slowly. "But I still don't see the answer."

"Let's try and think of another place near Salisbury with water and all that, and then fit it in with that line, if we can."

"It's an idea," nodded her sister. "Hotels, I think. It's not difficult, because there aren't very many of them just outside Salisbury."

"There's Newlands Park—that's about eight miles out," said Julie.

"Not even a swimming pool, though. That's out. What about Greenacres Park—that's got a big pool."

"But no dancing—it's purely residential," Julie pointed out.

Slowly and with considerable thought, the twins went one by one through all the hotels outside Salisbury. They consulted the telephone directory, and rang up the local Publicity Bureau to check the list.

It was the Publicity Bureau who finally produced one they had not thought of.

"It's only just opened," said the voice at the other end of the telephone. "Oval Vale. Residential—quite big. Swimming pool and a big dam, dining-room and the rest—dancing every Saturday evening. Is that all you want?"

"Yes, thanks," said Julie, happily, and rang off.

"We've got it," she whooped. "Oval Vale—it's only

about three miles out—off the main Lowland road. Oval Vale Hotel."

"Oval Vale," repeated June, thoughtfully. "Oval Vale—oh, what a rail."

"Rhyming slang," said Julie. "What a nasty one. Rhyming slang—Oval Vale—oh, what a rail!"

CHAPTER III

THE SECOND CLUE

"AND HAVING been sufficiently brilliant to solve the clue, what do we do now?" asked Julie, after a few moments.

"Why, we——" began June, and stopped.

Julie laughed.

"I know," she nodded. "We ring up our revered Parent, inform him that everybody else has the clue wrong, and we're the only ones that've got it right, and get him to let the police know so that they can bag Mr. X."

"Ye-es," agreed June, a little doubtfully.

"Exactly," said her twin. "And it doesn't sound a bit right, does it?"

"Well, after all, we've no idea if it is the right clue," argued June. "We might be right off the beam, and it might be McIlwaine, after all. And then everybody'd laugh at us."

"I quite agree. And, somehow, I think it'd be rather a shame to turn everybody loose on Mr. X."

"But he's a burglar!" exclaimed June.

"I know—but he sounds rather fun," said Julie, very earnestly. "I mean—he's a bit of a sport to give the police a clue to where he's going to—to operate next."

"Only if he plays fair, though," put in June cautiously.

"Yes, but I'm sure he will. He sounds that kind of person."

"Listen, my pet. Disabuse your mind of the idea that he's Errol Flynn or any of these gorgeous film stars having fun in a Hitchcock picture," said June, severely. "He's nothing but a common or garden thief."

"I don't—and I don't think so," explained Julie, a trifle obscurely. "What I mean is, I don't think he's a film star type, but I also don't think he's a common or garden thief. He wouldn't have worked out that clue if he had been, or written to the *Tribune* about it."

"So what?" asked her sister.

"So—I've got an idea. I won't be laughed at by everyone, and neither will you. So we can't possibly tell Father."

"And, if you think we're going to camp out at Oval Vale and c-c-capture the b-burglar single-handed, we're not, either," declared June.

"No, I know we can't. Besides, we're going to the Drive-In to-night, anyway."

"So—what's your idea?" asked June.

"I thought we might cycle up to Oval Vale—it's quite early and it wouldn't take us long. We'd be back long before Father got home."

"And then?"

"Well—we might leave a sort of note for Mr. X just in case it was the right place. Just to let him know we'd really solved it properly. It'd be rather fun—come on, June. Do say yes."

Julie knew from past experience that, although her sister would, on occasions, try and be firm-minded, she was just as keen on fun as Julie herself.

On previous occasions, a firm statement as to what fun a certain project would be had always conquered June's firm-mindedness.

On this occasion, it worked like a charm.

June's eyes lit up, she chuckled and nodded.

"You've got something there," she said. "The only snag is—just where do we leave the note? I mean, we can't walk up to the reception desk and leave it in an envelope addressed to Mr. X, can we?"

Julie frowned.

"I hadn't thought of that," she said. "I suppose there's not likely to be a blasted oak to be used as a letter box, as in all good adventure stories?"

"Not a chance," giggled June. "And don't use such bad language, either. You know the parents object to it."

"It's not bad language, it's a technical term," protested Julie. "Anyway—where can we leave it? Under a stone?"

"Pinned on to the gate-post?" suggested June.

"You might as well send it care of the *Tribune*," laughed Julie. "Seriously, where can we put it that he'll get it if he goes there this evening?"

"What about the obvious place—the notice-board?" asked June.

Her twin stared at her, mouth open.

"But—that's the last place, surely. Everybody'd see it except him," she said.

"It doesn't matter if everybody else sees it—all sorts of people are called Mr. X. Besides, it'd be quite a time before somebody's really curious enough to read it. You know perfectly well that nobody ever opens other people's letters."

"But—why should he see it? Why should he look at the notice-board—why should he be near it at all?" demanded Julie.

"Well, if he's going to steal something, he'll go upstairs to one of the hotel bedrooms, won't he?" said June, slowly. "And he's not very likely to do a cat-burglar stunt when it's so much simpler just to walk into the hotel through the main door. I mean, everybody else will be doing it, so why not be inconspicuous, just as though he were staying at the hotel?"

"Yes, that's all right so far. Go on," said Julie, encouragingly.

"Well, then. He strolls into the foyer as though he were a resident. And, as though he were a resident, he does what most of them do—glance at the letter-rack thing to see if there's any mail," finished June.

Julie frowned.

"I think it's a bit unlikely," she said.

"Well, you think of something better."

"I can't—that's the trouble," confessed Julie.

"In that case, let's try it. After all, if it doesn't work there's no harm done," said June.

"What do we want to say?" asked Julie.

"Simply that we think Oval Vale is the right clue, and that we've just been doing it for the fun of the thing. You know—we don't want to catch him or anything."

"Don't we?" asked Julie.

June pulled a face.

"I'd rather not," she said. "I think it'd be awful—sort of handing him over to the police, and then a court case and publicity and everything—it'd be horrible, wouldn't it?"

"I hadn't thought of it that way," agreed her twin. "You're quite right, of course. No, don't let's do anything about catching him. I mean, it's the job of the police, anyway. Let's just write him a note, and just sign it ' The Twins ' or something like that—not put our names or address on it, or anything. Then, if we're right, he'll know we're right, but we shan't get involved," she added, somewhat incoherently.

"All right," agreed June. "Let's do that now, and cycle up to the hotel and stick it on the board. It sort of ties it up nicely into a neat bow."

And the twins, without further discussion, got busy on the tying of the neat bow.

Having tied it, they cycled up to the hotel, which was a matter of three miles or so, left their cycles in the hotel porch, walked into the enormous hall, and unobtrusively tucked the letter addressed to Mr. X into one of the taped divisions on the big letter-board.

After which, they just as quietly walked out and cycled home, arriving in plenty of time to have tea and a bath before they changed to dine with their father and go to the Drive-In Cinema.

Late that evening, a small car—dark blue and of a popular make—was driven up to Oval Vale Hotel, and parked on the outskirts of the car park, bonnet pointing to the gates.

The driver, a tall young man dressed in grey flannels and a blazer with a well-known crest on the breast pocket, got out and, leaving the ignition key in its socket, strolled into the hotel.

Quietly, he made his way to the broad staircase that wound up to the first floor, and disappeared up the heavily carpeted flight.

Fifteen minutes later, he came down again equally quietly.

As he walked across the foyer, he casually glanced at the noticeboard.

Then he stopped dead, took a step nearer the board, and stared in obvious astonishment at the square white envelope addressed to ' Mr. X.'

He glanced round, but there were only a handful of people in the foyer.

A large, fat lady, dressed in a most unfortunate shade of purple, was arguing with the receptionist, while two girls, having obtained their room key, were waiting for the lift.

An elderly gentleman came into the hotel and walked up to the board, glanced at it, and took two letters from the lower corner. Then he turned and went over to the desk to collect his room key.

The tall young man evidently made up his mind, for

he quickly flicked the letter addressed to 'Mr. X' off the board, tucked it into his blazer pocket, and walked out of the hotel.

In a few moments he was in the small car and driving down the main road to Salisbury.

It was some time later that the young man pulled the letter out of his pocket.

He was, by then, sitting in a quiet corner of a popular café which kept open late, and was at the moment filled with the after-cinema crowd.

A cup of coffee in front of him, a cigarette between his fingers, he carefully studied the envelope. Then, turning it, he slit it open and pulled out the folded sheet of notepaper.

Unfolding it, he saw the writing was in a somewhat immature hand, though obviously an educated one, while both paper and envelope matched and were of a good quality.

His eyebrows lifted as he slowly read through the short letter and, by the time he had reached the signature, a smile was twitching at the corners of his mouth.

"*Dear Mr. X,*" he read. "*This is to let you know that we think your clue leads to Oval Vale Hotel and not to Lake McIlwaine, as everybody seems to think.*

"*We are not doing anything about it, though, because we don't really want to catch you as we shall then have to hand you over to the police, which would be a pity. We just had fun solving the clue, and we would like to thank you for that. It really was a stinker, but lots of fun.*

"*We do hope you will see this letter and realise it's*

for you, but if not, no harm will be done, whoever reads it.

"*Thanks again for the clue.*

Yours sincerely,

THE TWINS."

The young man read it through again. Then he folded the sheet and put it back into its envelope, before returning it to his pocket.

After which he sat smoking another cigarette thoughtfully. By the time he had finished the cigarette, he had evidently made up his mind, for he quickly stubbed it out in the ashtray, felt in his pockets and produced a pencil and a small memo-pad and began to scribble on a blank sheet of the pad.

Whatever he was writing evidently amused him for, as he finished it and read it through, he chuckled again.

Then, having paid his bill, he pocketed pad and pencil and left the café, turning to his left down the street which would eventually lead him to the offices of the *Tribune*.

The *Tribune* next morning printed an extra three thousand copies, and, even so, was sold out before midday.

That morning it was avidly read at every breakfast table throughout Greater Salisbury, and, for once, even the Civil Service was late arriving at its offices, due to the demands of the entire family to be allowed to read the paper.

The *Tribune* carried banner headlines right across its front page, and an amused public read that hundreds upon hundreds of people had spent most of the previous day solving the clue and interpreting it as meaning that Mr. X. would be at Lake McIlwaine Hotel.

The result was that at least half the happy solvers had decided to go and see for themselves, and the roads to the Lake had been jammed with cars full of happy burglar-hunters, and including children, dogs, and picnic baskets, all obviously prepared for a wonderful evening.

The fact that no burglar appeared, and only the police in some numbers were visible, apparently depressed nobody, for the lakeside cafés, whose proprietors had also solved the clue, flung wide their doors, and dances, boat trips on the lake and other amusements finally sent Salisbury residents cheerfully home at an extremely late hour.

While the *Tribune* readers were still chuckling that morning, their attention suddenly focused on a second headline drawing attention to another letter from Mr. X himself.

Addressed to the Editor of the *Tribune*, the writer apologised through the columns of the newspaper to all those who had so unfortunately misinterpreted the clue.

He went on to say that only two people had correctly solved it, and that the Lake Hotel had certainly not been his objective—in fact, it was, although a hotel, in quite a different part of the local country, in proof of which he had removed one single object from a certain room in that hotel, and later sent it to the police as a sign that he had, as he put it, played fair with police and public alike.

He added that he much regretted that it was unlikely that he would be in the burglaring business very much longer, thanked the public for their kind interest in his affairs and the clue, and was, the Editor's faithfully Mr. X.

Among the many thousands of eager readers were, naturally enough, the Twins.

Mr. Kennedy was a trifle surprised at their presence at the breakfast table since, during the school holidays, they normally appeared considerably later.

However, clad, certainly, in housecoats of vivid patterning, but undoubtedly washed and brushed, they were both eagerly reading the *Tribune* front page when he appeared at the table.

Indeed, so amused did they seem to be, and so interested in Mr. X, that Mr. Kennedy, really had not the heart to remove the newspaper from their grasp when he kissed them good-bye, and consequently had to buy another paper in town—which was no easy matter on that particular day.

He would have been even more surprised had he been able to hear their conversation after his departure.

"You see, we were right after all," said Julie, bouncing up and down to the excitement of the Dachshunds.

"Of course we were," agreed June, and the two laughed so much that Sausage and Mash fairly leapt up at them, barking furiously, to the utter disgust of Chang, who stalked towards the kitchen in the hope of finding a little peace there, and possibly a saucer of milk from Julius, who regarded the Siamese with a mixture of fear and superstitious wonder.

"And to think of everybody going out to McIlwaine, and only little us at the right place. We must be the two Mr. X is talking about, mustn't we, June?"

"I don't know," frowned June, sobering down a little. "There might have been two others and he just didn't know about us."

"He doesn't say how he knew about anybody getting the right place," said Julie, re-reading the letter.

"If he found that letter from us addressed to him, then we're the two," declared June.

"If he didn't, it must be still on the hotel board," said Julie, thoughtfully.

The twins stared at each other for a moment.

"D'you think we could telephone and ask if there's a letter for Mr. X?" asked Julie, a trifle nervously.

"It'd be a bit risky, wouldn't it?" asked June.

"I don't know—would it?" asked Julie.

The girls considered each other's questions.

"Everybody in the country knows now who Mr. X is," said Julie, at last. "If we ring up and ask for a letter addressed to Mr. X, won't they fall upon us immediately?"

"They can't do much on the phone, I don't think," said her sister.

"Supposing the phone is tapped. I've read about phones being tapped, and people listening in, I'm sure."

"That's what goes on in dictator countries, or whatever they're called," giggled June. "I'm sure they don't do that sort of thing here.   Don't forget, we're free, white and twenty-one here."

"Twenty one what?" asked Julie.

"Never mind. I should think it'd be quite safe to ring up the Hotel."

"It's the only way I can think of to find out if Mr. X got the letter. If he did, then we'll know we're the two. If it's still on the board, somebody else solved it as well as us."

"Just a minute, though," said June, quickly. "How would he know anybody else solved it?"

"Perhaps they wrote a note as well," suggested Julie, after a moment.

"You'll have the hotel board littered with letters to Mr. X in a minute," laughed June. "It's a point, though."

"Well, then, I don't know the answer. Anyway, the motion before the meeting is—to ring or not to ring."

"Oh, go on, telephone and ask," said June. "It can't do any harm. If they sound suspicious, all you do is to ring off, and since this is an automatic phone, they can't trace the call, anyway."

"All right," said Julie, a trifle doubtfully.

She picked up the telephone directory and hunted through it for the phone number of the Oval Vale Hotel, while June idly glanced through the remaining pages of the newspaper.

After a few moments, Julie found the number, and, picking up the receiver, dialled it and stood listening to the distant ringing tone.

"No answer," she said, briefly, after a few moments.

"Don't be silly—it's a hotel," answered June, absent-mindedly, as she studied the advertisement columns.

Julie waited a few moments longer.

Then there was a clunk at the other end of the line, as the receiver lifted, and a voice said: "Oval Vale Hotel. Good morning."

"Oh—er—good morning," said Julie, surprised.

"Can I help you?" asked the voice.

"Oh, yes. I wonder if you could tell me if there's a letter waiting for . . ." said Julie, and got no further.

With a shriek, June fairly leapt from her chair, rushed across to her sister, and banged the crossbar of the telephone down, cutting off the call.

Julie, receiver in hand, stared at her sister open-mouthed.

"What on earth——" she began.

"Look—look," said June, her voice high with excitement. "It's us. He got it. He's answered it. Oh, panjandrum, how clever we are—just look!"

Julie, in something of a daze, replaced the receiver and followed her sister across to the table.

For a moment she stared at the advertisement column which June was pounding with an agitated finger.

Then she suddenly saw it and bent to read it.

The next moment, the twins were dancing a wild fandango in the centre of the carpet, with the Dachshunds joining in shrilly.

When they calmed down slightly, they once again fell upon the newspaper and read the few lines in the Personal Column.

"*Twins—so glad you managed it. Try another. For sale where prickles do abound, things as such U lent and hope will be found. By smooth or rough proceed this way, and you will find profusion gay, certainly by the largest of them all, if you remember there to call. Good luck and have fun. X.*"

The twins read it through three times.

"It's certainly for us and from him," said Julie. "And a clue—but what a stinker."

"Now where have I heard that before?" asked June. "It's just like the other one. It doesn't mean a thing, to start with, at any rate."

"Where is it supposed to lead to?" demanded Julie. "I mean, is it another hotel, or a house, or what?"

"Could be anywhere," declared June. "It needn't be a house. Remember, he said in that letter to the *Tribune* that he was going out of the burglaring business. So it needn't be somewhere he wants to burgle."

Julie groaned.

"Here we go again—ice—wet towels—pencils and paper——"

"And Kit and Mollie are half-way to Inyanga by now," added June.

Julie looked up sharply.

"Good thing, too," she said. "We couldn't possibly let them in on this. No, darling, we've got to solve this all by ourselves."

"All right," agreed her twin. "Let's get dressed and then we can really get down to it."

An hour later, they were still struggling with the little verse.

"You know, I think it's a shop or something like that," declared Julie for the fifteenth time.

"Whoever heard of a shop selling prickles?" asked her twin, scornfully.

"What about a pet shop?" asked Julie suddenly, with dazzling brilliance.

" A pet shop?"

"Yes—prickles."

"Why prickles in a pet shop?" demanded June, exasperation in her voice.

"Prickles—hedgehogs—porcupines."

"M'm. It's an idea," nodded June. "But I'm certain you'd never find a hedgehog and certainly not a porcupine in a pet shop out here. They're wild game. You wouldn't find one in a pet shop even in England, would you?"

"I suppose not. Still, it was a good idea," said Julie.

" Oh, stupendous. Have several more, will you?"

"If I can," giggled Julie.

"What about a second-hand shop?" asked June.

"My turn, obviously. Why a second-hand shop?"

"Well, the lent bit. Things you lent."

"But you buy them in a second-hand shop," protested Julie.

"Well, you might not have—or whatever the wretched grammar is for that remark," retorted June. "You could have lent a book to somebody, and it got lost and it was eventually sold to a second-hand shop."

Julie wrinkled her forehead.

"It doesn't sound awfully probable to me," she said, slowly. "Anyway, we agreed that wherever it is must

be out of town, and I don't think you get second-hand
shops out of town."

"It could be an antique shop," suggested June.
"You often get them out of town—there's one near
Marandellas, remember?"

"It won't be as far as that," Julie pointed out.
"That's forty odd miles. And anyway, there's a good
deal of difference between a book you lent and a
Chippendale dining table."

"It needn't be a dining table, Chippendale or otherwise," said June, crossly.

"Must be something big—it says so. ' By the largest
of them all '."

"Sounds like a grandfather clock," grumbled June.
"The line I like best is the last one. Good luck and have
fun. That's sheer optimism and nothing else."

Julie laughed and poured out another glass of squash
for herself and one for June.

"Here you are, darling," she said. "This ought to
make you feel better."

"I doubt it. If we're not careful we'll be here till
lunch time without solving the wretched thing."

"I tell you what. Let's leave it for a bit and take
the dogs for a walk. That should clear our heads a
bit."

"That's a good idea," agreed June.

Sausage and Mash enthusiastically agreed, and in a
few moments all four were tearing across the lawn to
the gates.

By the time they had met some school friends and
talked for a while, shared two ice creams with the dogs,

who were quite as fond of ice cream as the girls, and eventually reached home, more than an hour and a half had gone by, and they flung themselves on the clue with renewed vigour.

At first, it seemed as difficult as ever, and then, suddenly, Julie was struck by a brilliant idea.

"I say, remember the pun in the first clue?" she asked. " About Oh, what a rail—you know, rhyming slang sort of thing."

"Yes," nodded June. "What about it?"

"Supposing he's done the same thing again in this one?"

"Why ever should he?"

"I don't know, but he might. Like the crossword people—if you do a lot that have been written or cross-worded or whatever it is by the same person, you get to know his mind and the way it works. We've often heard Father say that of the *Tribune* crossword."

"Yes, that's right. 'Member how cross he was when they changed people and he couldn't get one out for weeks?" giggled June.

"Well, perhaps there's the same sort of thing in this second clue," went on Julie.

"I don't see anything that looks like rhyming," declared June. "Nothing possible rhymes with prickles or lent or anything like that."

"I'm sure there's a trick with that capital U," said Julie, frowning heavily. " Otherwise it'd be the proper spelling of you."

"Printer's error—there are always some in advertise-ments," said her sister.

"I don't think so this time. It's the key, I'm sure. Such U lent. Such U lent."

"There's no sense in that—such U lent," said June, mockingly.

"Such U lent—succulent," repeated June. "But you never lend succulents—that's cactus and prickly stuff."

"Prickly—you've got it," howled Julie. "Prickles—prickles do abound—succulents."

"Ye-es," began June. "Then——"

"Succulents—cactuses—cacti, I mean," went on Julie, talking at the top of her voice. "What's the place—the gardens—where they grow the things—you know——"

"Ewanrigg," said June. "Of course—oh, you're brilliant. Ewanrigg—the cacti gardens—and all we've got to do is to find the largest."

"That's right. The road's tarred nearly all the way now—just a bit of the old dirt road left near the end, I think. How far is it? We've never been there before."

"It's only about ten miles or so out," said June, excitedly. "We'll ask Father to lend us the Vane this afternoon—he's home to lunch."

"Will he, d'you think?" asked Julie.

"Of course he will," said June, firmly. "We'll tell him we want to improve our education by a visit to Ewanrigg—he won't mind. He's often said we ought to go and look at it—it's a show place. He'll let us, and we can drive out after lunch."

The sisters fell on each other in an access of delight,

and only Julius, putting his head round the door to say lunch was ready and the Boss was just coming in, brought them to their senses.

Then they rushed off to tidy before appearing at lunch.

June was perfectly correct in saying that Mr. Kennedy did not mind lending them the car.

He was always a trifle cautious, but on such an occasion, when he did not require it himself, he said that they could certainly have it, and handed over the keys to June, only asking them to drive him back to the office before going to Ewanrigg to improve their education.

The twins hurried through lunch, and then scampered away to change into crisp, summer frocks and clean white sandals before rejoining Mr. Kennedy in the garden, where he was drinking his after-lunch coffee.

By two o'clock they had dropped him at his office, and June was turning the car in the direction of Ewanrigg, the enormous garden famous throughout the world for its vast collection of cacti and succulents of every description, which had been gathered over many years by a succession of experts.

" Oh, I do think this is exciting," said Julie, giving a little wriggle.

"It'll be even more exciting if I can't get past this brute of a lorry," said June. "I'm slowly dying of asphyx-whatever it is from the exhaust fumes of the thing."

"It's one of the Kariba Transport lorries—what

monsters they are!" exclaimed Julie. "Go on, now. The road's clear ahead."

June changed down expertly and shot ahead past the vast trailer which swung perilously behind the almost equally vast lorry.

Then the road was clear, and they went sailing up a hill and down the other side.

The road was bordered on either side by white, single-story houses, built in the Spanish style, with wide stoeps, and with large gardens in which red, pink and yellow poinsettias, leafless but in full bloom, vied with the many-shaded bougainvillaea bushes.

Presently, they came to a large signpost, and obediently swung off the main, tarred road, on to a smooth, dirt road, and were soon at the gates of Ewanrigg.

There were a few cars parked outside, but, since it was a week-day, there were none of the usual crowds, and the twins had no difficulty in finding a convenient place to leave the car.

"Now for the largest cactus we can find," murmured Julie, as they walked through the gates.

"I wonder where we start," laughed June, gazing at the grounds which stretched ahead of them.

"We'll have to ask somebody, I expect," suggested Julie. "Anyway, let's have a look round first."

They walked slowly down the wide path, and, as they passed a huge clump of tall green succulents, a young man stepped up to them. He lifted his hat, looked at them and smiled.

"Excuse me," he said in a pleasant voice. "You're the twins, aren't you?"

The girls stared at him.

"We're twins, certainly," said Julie, coldly. "But I'm afraid we don't know what you mean by *the* twins."

"All right," said the young man. "I'll take a chance. I think you're the Twins. I think you're looking for something. And, if you are, perhaps this is it—under the largest succulent you or I have ever seen!"

And he offered them a small oblong envelope, addressed to ' The Twins'.

CHAPTER IV

NIGHT STOP

THE TWINS stared first at the envelope and then at the young man.

"Are you—are you Mr.——" began Julie, and then swallowed hastily and was silent.

"Mr. X?" asked the young man. "I'm sorry to disappoint you, but I'm not."

"M-m-mr. X?" stammered June, in a rather vain attempt to retrieve the situation. "W-w-who's Mr. X?"

"Oh, come now," laughed the young man. "You can't—you simply can't get away with that one. There's not a man, woman or child in Salisbury, and probably in the Rhodesias, who doesn't know about Mr. X. by now."

"Oh—Mr. X," gulped June. "Oh, yes, of course. We've—we've heard of Mr. X."

"I bet you have," said the young man. "By the way, hadn't you better take this envelope?"

"Oh—well er——" stammered Julie. "Is—is it for us?"

"I should think so," he replied, rather drily. "It's addressed to you, isn't it?"

Julie took a deep breath and pulled herself together.

"Well—perhaps," she said. "And perhaps not."

"That certainly clears up the position nicely," said

the young man. "Look here," he added, suddenly. "There's a refreshment place over there. Suppose we stagger that far and have a cup of coffee or something, while you get yourselves organised."

"Well——" began June, doubtfully.

"I think perhaps it's a good idea," said Julie, quickly. "Mind you, we still don't know whether that's for us, but——"

"But you are twins, of course. I quite understand," said the young man, and led them to the small rondavel with thatched roof and open sides, where several small tables were clustered together, and a little counter was neatly set out with cups and saucers and sugar basins.

They were soon served by the usual, white-clad African, and there were a few moments of silence, while they stirred their coffee thoughtfully and glanced sideways at each other.

Then the young man lit a cigarette, blew out a cloud of smoke, and spoke.

"Well, are we going to unbosom ourselves to each other?" he asked, blandly. "Are you going to tell me about Mr. X?"

"We don't know anything about Mr. X," said Julie, firmly.

"Oh, come now. If you know nothing about him, why did you ask if I was Mr. X? And why did you think that envelope was for you?"

"Well—you said were we twins, and——" began June.

"Look," cut in the young man. "We're not going to get anywhere this way. Suppose we decide to open up a bit, eh? I'll tell you why I want to know about Mr. X, and you tell me why he's writing to you and posting the letters here. Agreed?"

The twins looked at each other for a moment. Then they nodded.

"All right," agreed June.

"Good," said the young man.

"You start," said Julie, quickly. "Start by telling us who you are—and why you're interested in Mr. X."

"Fair enough," he nodded. "Though I could say everybody in the place is interested in Mr. X."

"But you more than most," said June.

"Agreed. All right, we'll start off with me. First of all, my name's Terry Davidson. Secondly, I'm in the police—C.I.D. Now don't get scared," he added quickly, as the twins glanced at each other, and turned a little pale.

"A policeman!" exclaimed Julie.

"Well, it's not as bad as that," said Terry. "I mean, I'm not going to arrest you and whisk you off to prison, or anything like that. Quite the other way round. I want your help—that's all."

"Oh, we can't possibly help you," said Julie, quickly.

"You don't know till you've listened to me," said Terry, calmly.

"Oh, yes, we do," said June. "You want us to help you to find Mr. X, don't you. And we couldn't possibly do that."

"Why not?" asked the detective.

"Well, we—er—we couldn't. That's all," she replied.

"We don't know anything about him," added Julie.

"Yet he's writing you letters and you've come out

here to pick up this one, haven't you?" said the detective.

Julie flushed.

"He's not writing us letters," she flashed. "And we don't know anything about him. We've never seen him, even. We can't help you at all—and I think we'd better be going."

"Just a minute," said the young man, as she started to get up. "Just listen to me for a minute. I don't know what sort of an idea you have of this Mr. X, but I'd like to point out something to you. He's not the Scarlet Pimpernel or Raffles or any of these rather glamorous fiction types. Mr. X is a thief—a plain, straightforward criminal. A thief who goes into a private house and helps himself to something that doesn't belong to him; jewellery—very valuable jewellery. Some of the stuff he stole were heirlooms—family heirlooms with a great deal of sentimental value attached to them—irreplaceable from that point of view, because you can buy other jewellery with the insurance money, but you cannot replace brooches, bracelets, a locket that belonged to your great-grandmother, let us say. And Mr. X trespassed—entered a private house—and helped himself. Just bear that in mind when you read the rather rose-coloured accounts of the gay, light-hearted Mr. X, with his amusing verses and his witty clues."

There was a long silence.

"Yes, I see what you mean," said June at last.

"Of course, we hadn't looked at it that way," added Julie, slowly.

"That's all right," smiled the detective. "I'm sure you hadn't—that's why I thought I'd better just put the other side of the picture in front of you. Not your fault, of course. It's only too easy to get misled in a thing like this."

"Before we tell you what we know about Mr. X—and it's not much, I'm afraid," said Julie, and stopped.

"Go on," encouraged the young man.

"Well, before we do tell you, would you tell us something?"

"Of course."

"How did you know about that letter—and about us—and Ewanrigg?"

Terry Davidson laughed.

"That's easy," he said, lighting another cigarette. "I'm one of the many lesser lights that have been on the outskirts of this Mr. X business. Don't get me wrong," he added, earnestly. "I don't want you to think I'm one of the Big Five, or that I always get my name in the papers because of the big cases I solve or anything like that. I'm just a common or garden, underpaid, overworked member of the C.I.D.—very downtrodden and inconspicuous and of little consequence. In fact, I'm only employed to do the donkey work."

The twins were laughing at him.

"We don't believe you, really, but go on," said June.

"Well, in my spare time I read the newspapers," he went on, solemnly. "Not ' Around the Courts ' or anything morbid like that, but the cartoons, the strips, the gossip column and the advertisements—particularly hatch, match and dispatch and——"

"The *what*?" demanded Julie.

"Sorry—slip of the tongue. Births, Marriages and Deaths—just to see who I know who's been born or something. And, above everything else, the Personal Column. I've a weakness for the Personal Column. I love those messages to Ken from Pen saying Mum not happy come home at once. Or the Meet-you-under-the clock-Saturday ones."

"Oh, I see," said June. "And so you saw the clue addressed to the Twins and signed X."

"That's it in a nutshell."

"But—how did you get any further than that?" asked Julie.

"It struck me that the verse was remarkably like that McIlwaine clue. Coupled, of course, with the X. And, by much good fortune and my own brilliant brain, I managed to solve it. So I took a chance and half a day's leave and came out to look for twins. When I saw you—well, that's as far as we've got."

"One more thing," said Julie. "What about Oval Vale?"

"Hush!" said Terry. "We don't mention it if there's a copper within earshot. Nobody thought of anything but the Lake."

"And it really was Oval Vale," said June.

"Oh, yes. Mr. X obliged us with details. Just for the book, he'd helped himself to a diamond wrist-watch from room 13 which he obligingly returned to us

It all tied up, and he certainly was there. And now it's your turn. What d'you know about Mr. X."

"I told you it was very little," warned Julie. "Of course, you know it was us that solved the clue as Oval Vale. We didn't know what to do about it then, and nobody would have believed us if we'd said Oval Vale, because apparently even the police knew for certain it was the Lake. So we wrote a note to Mr. X saying we thought it was Oval Vale, and then we addressed it to him, and cycled out to the hotel, and stuck it on the board for letters in the foyer of the hotel."

Terry Davidson was staring at them, open-mouthed, his cigarette dangling from his fingers. In fact, it was not until the cigarette burnt his fingers that he moved at all.

With a smothered exclamation, he stubbed it out and looked at the twins again.

"You—just—wrote to him, cycled out and left the note—addressed to Mr. X—on the hotel letter-board for all to see?" he demanded.

"That's right," nodded the twins.

"We didn't put our name or address or anything in it, and we signed it The Twins," added June.

"And what did you say in this note?" asked Terry.

"Just that we thought this was the right clue, and we'd had fun solving it, and that sort of thing," said Julie, calmly.

"But how did you know he'd get it?" demanded Terry.

"Oh, we didn't," giggled Julie. "But we just took a chance that he might see it if he was pretending to be an ordinary guest at the hotel, and if he didn't it wouldn't matter, anyway, because there was no name or address on it."

"Well—blow me down," said Terry, inelegantly, and lit another cigarette.

Then he ran his fingers through his fair, somewhat curly hair, and ordered another cup of strong coffee.

"So what then?" he asked.

"That's all," said Julie. "We saw that advertisement in the Personal Column this morning, and of course we knew we'd been right about Oval Vale, and that he must have found our note. So we spent the morning solving the rhyme—it was a shocker, too, wasn't it?— and—well, here we are."

"And here you are," agreed Terry, weakly. "You know, you two shouldn't be allowed out alone."

"I don't see why," retorted June. "We're perfectly harmless."

"That's a matter of opinion," said Terry. "Anyway, what next?"

"Well, if that's another clue, we open it," said Julie, and looked at Terry very hard.

"I see," he said, slowly. "But what I don't understand is—why these last clues?"

"What d'you mean?" asked June.

"Well, the first clue was open to all comers," explained Terry. "Fair enough. You solved it—also fair enough. But then Mr. X sends you a second clue—he publishes it in an advertisement for you to see. And, when you've solved that, there's still another clue. Where's it all leading to?"

"There may not be a clue in that envelope," said June, eyeing the envelope which lay in the centre of the table between the three of them. "It may be a note or—well, anything."

"Yes, I see," said Terry, quietly.

Then he flicked the envelope across to the twins.

"You'd better open it and find out," he said, briefly.

The twins sat quite still.

"Don't you want to find out what's in it?" he asked, after a moment. "Or—don't you want me to know?"

"It's—our clue," said Julie. "And although we agree with all you've said about Mr. X, and of course we know you're right, still——"

Her voice trailed away, but June nodded.

"It's just that—just that it seems a bit mean—sort of betraying Mr. X, you see," she explained. "I mean, he wrote that to us in all good faith, and if it helped you to catch him, it'd—well, it'd leave a nasty feeling inside us."

Terry stifled an exasperated sigh.

"All right," he said. "Have it your own way. I'm not going to argue with you any more or try and make you see the error of your ways. But I'd like to make a bargain with you, if you'll agree."

The twins looked at him a little nervously.

"It's quite simple," he went on. "It's just this. Let me in on this treasure hunt of yours—let me string along with you, just to make certain you're safe and you don't come to any harm. And, in return, I'll keep you in the picture from my side. I'll always tell you what I'm doing, and, if we look like laying hands on Mr. X through you, I'll let you know first—what do you say?"

The twins looked at him and then at each other.

"Why are you doing that?" asked Julie.

Terry smiled.

" D'you agree?" he said. "It lets you out of having a nasty feeling about him, doesn't it?"

"Ye-es, I think so," nodded June. "And it's jolly decent of you."

"Yes," agreed Julie. "I know we're being tiresome, and, of course, you're perfectly right about him being a burglar and all that—I think it's pretty nice of you. I think we'll agree, don't you?"

June nodded agreement.

" And now please answer my question," went on Julie. "Why are you doing it?"

"I'll tell you," said Terry. "In strict confidence, the police have got lots of clues, but they don't seem to be very profitable ones. There's a terrific hate on from the high-ups about incompetence and not being able to catch a simple thief, and all that. And we're pretty stuck. Now you at least are in touch with him—so you're my best lead. Nobody else is on to anything much yet, and if I can manage to get alongside him, it'll be bells and shouts of joy for me."

"But you won't catch him through us," protested Julie. "You've just said you'll tell us before you do anything, and that'll give us time to warn him."

"You never know," said Terry, lightly. "You warn him as much as you like. I'll take a chance on collecting him just the same. And now what about it? Will you open the envelope and let me know the worst?"

The sisters agreed, and Julie quickly ripped open the envelope and pulled out the card that was inside.

"Just listen to this," she said, and read aloud what was written on the card.

"*Dear Twins*," it ran. "*I hope you're having fun still. You seem to like solving clues, so I thought a little treasure hunt might enliven your obviously rather dull school holidays. Hence this clue. It's not as bad as some. There'll probably be another one or two and then a small prize for two bright girls, perhaps. Happy solving.*

Mr. X."

"Doesn't sound much like a thief," frowned Terry. "May I see it?"

"Just a minute—the clue's on the back," said Julie. "Oh, golly, just listen."

She turned over the card, and her eyes were wide as she read the few lines.

"*Proceed from hence to the aqua plain, where combing of hair is not thought vain. Where total immersion is done a lot and letters H to O are on the spot. Hurry there and you will find clues and drinks come from behind.*"

"He's the most extraordinary burglar I've ever heard of," said Terry, as he took the card from Julie's fingers and studied it.

"Why?" asked June.

"It's written on good quality card and envelope in educated handwriting, and he's obviously had a first-class education," explained Terry. "Besides which, what ordinary sort of crook goes in for this kind of caper? Setting rhymed clues and organising what he calls a treasure hunt for two youngsters he knows nothing about and has never met—unless he's a friend of yours, and a thief on the quiet," he added.

" Oh, we don't know him at all," chorused the sisters.

"I don't get it," said Terry, shaking his head. "I don't get it at all. That burglary was the work of an ordinary crook. This isn't. This is quite different. But I wish I knew why."

He ran his fingers through his hair and stared at the card again.

"Perhaps you'll find out when we've reached the last clue," said Julie. "Meanwhile, we think it's frightfully exciting—a real treasure hunt all to ourselves."

"Rather," agreed June. "It's like that game we play at parties, where you find a clue and that leads you to another and another, and when you've got them all, you win a prize."

" And we'll win no prizes at all if we don't solve this one," added Julie.

"He says it's not difficult," said June. "Let's take it bit by bit."

" All right," giggled Julie. "Where's an aqua plain?"

"Lake McIlwaine, perhaps," said June, with a laugh.

"Not that sort of plane," scoffed her sister. "Plain—plain as opposed to fancy. Not gaudy. Plain."

" Oh, like the ones in the Wild West," said June. "There aren't any plains round this part of the world—only plateaux according to our geography mistress. Anyway, why comb your hair on a plain?"

"I suppose you can comb your hair anywhere you

like," said Julie. "But that doesn't tie up with the bit about being vain. It's not vain to comb your hair, is it?"

"Not that I've ever heard of," said her sister. "We're not getting on very fast. What's the next line?"

"Total immersion," said Julie. "It sounds like a laundry. And H to O might be a crossword clue, or one of those puzzles with dots in between to show you how many letters are missing."

" And it finishes with clues and drink coming from behind—behind what?" demanded her sister.

"Who said this was easy," giggled Julie.

Terry was lighting another cigarette and frowning thoughtfully at the small flame of his silver cigarette lighter.

"Can you solve it?" asked Julie, and he jumped slightly, flicked off his lighter and slipped it into a pocket.

"Who—me?" he asked. "Not on your life. I've always avoided crossword puzzles. I turn off the radio when there's a quiz programme on, and I tear out the puzzle page in the Sunday supplement and throw it away."

"In other words, you don't like puzzles," said Julie, solemnly.

"You have it in a nutshell," he agreed. "Consider me as a broken reed. I can't spell, to start with, which is no help with anagrams, crosswords, acrostics or any other inventions of the devil. I can't add up properly, because I invariably include the date or the number I first thought of. I get three different answers and choose the middle one, which is usually wrong, so I can't do the sort of thing that tells you somebody has so much change less half-a-crown, plus what he had before he spent what he thought he hadn't got when he left home."

"The answer's always twice the original sum, less what he discovered in his other pocket that his wife had overlooked," explained June, solemnly.

"Is it? Thank you," said Terry, equally gravely. "I'll remember that for the future. In the meantime, suppose you get on and solve that clue. It's getting late, and I'm not supposed to be out after dark."

"We're not getting on very fast," explained Julie. "What with plain aqua—as different from coloured, I suppose—combs and laundries, it's not terribly easy."

"The clue's in those wretched letters again, I'm sure," said June. "He runs true to form. H to O. Like Such-U-lent. Only without a pun, as far as I can see."

For about fifteen minutes, the twins worried over the clue, scribbling down words here and there on the back of the envelope with the pencil they had borrowed from Terry, while he smoked more cigarettes and drank a third cup of coffee.

Finally, he stubbed out his cigarette, pushed his coffee cup aside and leant across the table.

"I can't make up my mind whether I'm turning into a dried tobacco leaf or a coffee grain," he said. "But, since I'd rather be neither, supposing I offer a slight— a very slight—suggestion."

The sisters looked at him attentively.

"Go on," they urged leaning forward in their chairs.

"June said that those two letters H to O were probably the clue," he went on. "But you haven't really followed that up, have you?"

"Haven't we just?" snorted Julie. "We've been through the whole blessed alphabet between them, and a bit on each side for good measure. But it doesn't make a bit of sense."

"You're falling down on the adverb," said Terry.

"The adverb? There's no adverb—it's a couple of consonants," said Julie, indignantly.

"Education—here I come," said Terry, rolling his eyes to the sky. "Adverb—dear child—Adverb meaning a word that qualifies or modifies an adjective, verb or other adverb, expressing a relation of place, time, circumstance, manner, etc., and points North. I learnt that at my mother's knee," he added with a smirk.

"Well, now we know. Thanks very much. It's a great help," said Julie, crossly. "But just where does it get us."

"Consider—consider that when he writes 'to', he's only foxing you—you mentioned a pun, didn't you? Well, then—he doesn't mean 'to'—he means 'two'," said Terry, triumphantly.

The twins looked nervously at him.

"When he writes to, he doesn't mean to, he means to," repeated Julie, after a moment. "Oh, I see what you mean. And thank you very much. And now I really think we'll have to be going—if you'll excuse us——"

Terry chuckled.

"It's all right—I'm not crackers," he said. "Give me that pencil."

June handed it to him.

"Now," he said, turning the envelope over to find a blank space. "That is written H to O, isn't it. But supposing it should really be H_2O. See what I mean?"

The twins stared at the writing.

"H_2O," said Julie. "Water!"

"Aqua!" exclaimed June. "And total immersion and all—oh, you're brilliant!"

She flung Terry a beaming smile, and turned to her sister.

"How stupid of us—of course, it's the baths—the swimming baths. You comb your hair there, when you've finished swimming. And there's a lot of total immersion—and H_2O's certainly on the spot—gallons and gallons of it."

"That's right. And the drinks and things come from the tea room place. How idiotic we were not to think of it before," cut in Julie. "The swimming baths. Come on, let's go there right away and get the next clue."

The three stood up, the twins fairly dancing with excitement.

"We've never been so quick before," said Julie.

"We shouldn't have been now if it hadn't been for you," added June. "Are you coming with us to the baths?"

"Try stopping me," grinned Terry. "I've got my own car here—I'll follow you, shall I?"

Chattering excitedly, the twins walked out of the cactus gardens with the detective.

He saw them into their car, and waited while Julie started up the engine, slipped into gear, steered the car on to the road, and started off at a good pace for Salisbury and the big swimming bath in the centre of the town.

Then he climbed into his own elderly, shabby and extremely fast M.G. and followed them.

The girls reached the baths in record time, and pulled up in the car park, the M.G. next to them.

Then they all got out and walked through the railings placed at intervals across the wide gravel road to prevent cars being taken right up to the doors.

They climbed the flight of steps leading to the entrance—and stopped dead.

In front of them, barring their way, were the tall gates. They were firmly padlocked. The swimming bath had closed for the night.

Furiously, Julie shook the gates, but they were quite firm. Peering through them, she could see the enormous swimming pool, its water quite still, not a ripple on the surface. Along each side, the wide paved borders were empty. Nobody sat on the benches or lounged on the grass in the setting sun.

There was no doubt about it—the baths were closed and there was no sign of any person.

Terry, exasperated, let out a shout, and the twins yodelled once or twice.

But the only person to appear was an African attendant, cleaning rag in hand.

"The Boss? The Superintendent? Where's the Boss?" demanded Terry through the gates.

The African slowly shook his head and blinked at them.

"Is no one here, Boss," he said. "Boss going towndi. Come back mangi-mangi. Ten o'clock— 'leven o'clock——"

He shrugged his shoulders and turned away, and disconsolately the three walked down the steps, knowing that nothing more could be done until the next day.

CHAPTER V

ENTER A. N. OTHER

THERE WAS quite obviously nothing to be done for the rest of the day, and the twins, having arranged with Terry that he should collect them at about half-past eight the following morning, when they could all go to the swimming baths together and find the clue, drove slowly home.

They pulled up outside the gate, and for a moment or two sat staring at the dappled sunlight patterning the roadway.

"About to-morrow," began Julie, at last.

Her sister glanced at her.

"Yes?" she said.

"Supposing—well, supposing we find the clue and—and decipher it—and—and it tells us where to find Mr. X—where to meet him or how to get in touch with him—you know," said Julie.

"Well—supposing?" said June, quietly.

"Well," echoed Julie. "What I mean is—d'you think it's—it's going to be difficult?"

"Difficult? You mean because Terry will be with us," said June, slowly.

"Yes. I mean, supposing we find out how to contact Mr. X—it might be—awkward—for him—if he only thought he was telling us and—somebody else found out—or——" went on Julie.

"You mean, Terry Davidson," said her sister. "I agree with you."

"Oh, that's a relief," laughed Julie. "I was bit afraid that I was being queer and fussy."

"No fear. I'm with you all along the line. I know that everything he said about burglars and going into private houses and family heirlooms and all that was quite correct. And I quite agreed with it. But still——"

"Exactly," nodded Julie. "But still. I wish we could let Mr. X know in some way that we've got mixed up with the police, and that we're afraid of involving him."

"How can we? We've no idea how to get hold of him. He's certainly not likely to go to Oval Vale again, and that was the only place we really contacted him, wasn't it."

"I'm sure we ought to do something," said Julie. "Otherwise, however careful we are, we're going to give the whole thing away somehow, somewhere."

"I don't see how we can, but I quite agree with you. And that brings us back to where we started. Although we agree with Terry, we don't want to give Mr. X away."

"I don't see even how Terry telling us beforehand what he's going to do will help, do you?" added Julie, morosely. "I mean, if we can't get hold of Mr. X to tell him or warn him, what does it matter what Terry tells us?"

"It's a mess," nodded her sister. "I wish there was some way of letting him know about Terry."

"There *must* be a way," said Julie, desperately. "Let's think hard—there must be a way."

For five long minutes the twins sat staring dolefully out of the windscreen.

A child ran by, laughing at the puppy that ran with it. Three doves flew down to land gracefully in the road and strut to and fro, pecking at invisible insects. A black cat watched them sombrely, knowing how useless it was to try and attempt to catch one.

Julie gave a deep sigh.

"I give up," she said. "My brain's seized up completely. Short of asking the Federal Broadcasting Corporation to put out an S.O.S. after the news to-night, I've no idea what to do. And even that isn't very good, because he might not be listening to the radio. He might be at the bioscope instead."

"Then you'd better play safe and ask the managers of the three cinemas to put it on the screen as well, just to make sure," giggled her sister.

"I still think there must be something we can do," said Julie doggedly. "I know we've no idea what he's like, where he lives or works or anything—it's all completely one-sided, because he could well know what we look like."

"How?"

"He might have watched us this afternoon at Ewanrigg, after he'd planted the clue," suggested Julie. "There were quite a number of people strolling around during the afternoon."

"Then he'd have seen Terry with us, and guessed what had happened."

"That won't work," Julie said, shaking her red curls. "For all he knows, Terry could have been a cousin or a brother or a friend or anybody."

"*Not* a relation, per-lease," smiled June. "He's not got red hair, and he's not in the least like us."

"Distant branch of the family who married into the Scandinavians and ran true to form with fair hair, blue eyes. Tallish, too," said Julie, absent-mindedly. "And, even if Mr. X doesn't know what we look like, he will probably check to see if we found the clue. Anyway, he knows he can always get us through the Personal Column if he wants to——"

She stopped, turned her head and stared at her sister who was staring back at her.

"The Personal Column," she repeated, softly.

"That's it," agreed June. "We can put in an ad. right away."

In considerable excitement, Julie scrabbled through the inevitable tangle of things that always seemed to find their way to the ledge under the dashboard of the car.

There was a pencil—but the point was broken. Another, very short, but with some lead visible, so that was all right.

Now something to write on—and she fumbled for the small notebook which her mother always insisted on having in the car, ever since the day she had wanted to leave Mr. Kennedy a message in the car, and could only find a handkerchief on which to write it, and only a lipstick for a pencil.

Maps, dog leads, a rather oily duster, three or four nails and a small pocket screwdriver in a worn leather case, a torch battery, obviously used, some string, a small, incredibly sticky roll of black insulating tape:

"I know it's here somewhere," she muttered, as June also fingered through the surprising assortment.

A tin of sweets, almost empty, a penknife which June had lost weeks before, odds and ends of crumpled paper—and then, at last, Julie emerged triumphant with the small scribbling pad.

"What do we say?" she asked, and the two girls put their heads together to evolve something which would not be too incriminating, and would yet meet the eye of Mr. X.

Eventually, Julie read out the finished result.

"I think this'll do," she said. "Listen. ' *Mr. X. Clue spotted. Thanks a lot. Copper influence rather heavy. The Twins*'."

"Sounds like news from the Copperbelt," said June, with a laugh. "But I think it's a bit obvious. Suppose Terry spots that?"

"Yes, he could turn rather nasty, and that'd be a pity," agreed Julie. "But what else can we say?"

"I don't think we ought to put: ' Mr. X '. Lots of people might guess that it's meant for him, and goodness knows what trouble there'd be, then. They might be able to trace the advertisement back to us."

"I hadn't thought of that," said Julie. "We'd better

not, then. But how can we make him recognise the message any other way?"

"Just by signing it—The Twins?" suggested June.

"I think that could be dangerous, too," said Julie.

"I've got it," cried June, excitedly. "I know—look, start again. Put in that bit about the copper influence. Don't mention anything about a clue. Just thanks. And then let's quote the swimming bath clue. He'll recognise that and it won't mean a thing to anybody else."

"Why, that's brilliant," said Julie, and hurriedly turned to a fresh sheet of paper. "I'll start. ' *Thanks. Copper influence rather heavy.*' And then I'll quote the clue."

In a few moments, the whole matter satisfactorily settled, June drove to the offices of the *Tribune*, and between them they wrote the advertisement out neatly on one of the special printed forms provided for that purpose.

Then they marked it carefully for one insertion only the following morning, and handed it in to the clerk behind the little window labelled in large type ' Small Advertisements '.

"You could put in lines and lines and lines of advertisement, and it'd still be small," giggled Julie.

The clerk frowned and adjusted his glasses.

"It's not a matter of the size of an advertisement, it's not that at all," he said, reprovingly. "It's a question of difference, you see? Difference, that's what it is."

"Oh, I see," said Julie, politely.

"It's the difference between displayed ads and

smalls," went on the clerk earnestly. "They're display ads when they're displayed in the paper, you see? Displayed, that's what they are, displayed meaning set out, like the shop advertisements are, see? Spread all over the paper they are, sometimes, spread all over. But smalls are always smalls, see?"

The twins agreed that they saw, and the clerk studied the advertisement they had handed him.

"Nice bit of poetry," he said, as he came to the end of the advertisement. "Walt Whitman, isn't it?"

"Er—well—probably," stammered June, taken by surprise.

"I read a bit of Walt Whitman once," said the clerk, marking curious hieroglyphics on the form. "Fond of poetry, I am, very fond of it. Not long stuff, mind you, but bits here and there—well, there's nothing like poetry at times, is there, nothing like it? Two and threepence."

Julie realised with a start that the last three words referred to the price, and produced half a crown from her pocket.

"This'll be in the Smalls to-morrow morning," he said, handing her a tickey change. "Personal Column, as marked, but still Smalls—all single column, small type, straightforward stuff is smalls, as I told you, you see?"

The twins hurriedly saw, thanked him and fairly ran out of the office, to collapse in strangled gasps of mirth in the car.

All the way home, they referred to smalls, poetry, and Walt Whitman see, and were still at the giggling stage when they finally turned the car into the garage.

Mr. Kennedy was already at home, so they pulled themselves together, and were soon sitting comfortably in the garden having tea with their father.

Mr. Kennedy usually left the house about eight o'clock in the morning, and the twins were dressed and waiting when the M.G. drew up with a noisy chug-chug of the exhaust, and a subdued blare on the horn.

Sausage and Mash, who objected on principal to such noises, tore out of the house, skidded off the stoep, and raced across the garden, ears streaming behind them, their ridiculous paws paddling at top speed, shrieking at the tops of their voices.

Terry, who had got out of the car, fairly leapt for the safety of the driver's seat, and only just made it in time. He sank down and made rude noises at them, driving them to a frenzy of barking and scrabbling at the outside of the car.

The twins eventually managed to call them to order, and apologised to their visitor.

"They're usually very well behaved," said June. "They never bite anybody."

"I'm very glad of that," said Terry, solemnly.

"They just didn't realise that you're a friend of ours," said Julie. "Look, Mash. This is Terry. Terry's a friend. You must be a good dog with Terry. Understand? Nice Terry."

Mash looked at Terry with bright eyes, and his red lips curled back to show as fine a set of large, sharp-looking white teeth as Terry had ever seen.

"Er—could we skip the brother-to-brother act?" he

asked, drawing back hurriedly. "And, if you've got a house-trained lion or two, I'd just as soon not bother with meeting it at the moment."

"Oh, he is naughty!" exclaimed Julie. "I'm awfully sorry. I can't imagine what's the matter with him."

"Don't try," begged Terry, earnestly.

Sausage, struggling in his mistress's arms, was growling and grumbling at the bottom of his voice.

"Yes, and we'll skip the introductions with that little lamb, too, if you don't mind," he added, and made a face at Sausage which sent him into hysterics of rage.

"W-won't you come in?" asked June, trying not to laugh.

"I don't think so, thanks," replied Terry. "I'm rather fond of this pair of trousers, and I'd just as soon keep them intact, if it's all the same to you."

"Oh, you're perfectly safe. They never——" began June.

"Oh, I'm quite sure they don't. But, all the same, I'd rather not try just now. If you could muzzle them, or chain them up, or put them in a cage or something, we could sort of sneak away before they broke loose again, couldn't we?"

Trying to keep straight faces, the twins hurriedly went off to shut up the little dogs, instructing a grinning Julius to release them once the car had gone, and then ran back to the M.G.

In a few moments, they had climbed in, and Terry was sending the car snorting down the street.

This time, when they arrived at the swimming baths, the gates were folded back, the pay-desk window was open, and shouts and splashes came from the big pool itself where half a dozen youngsters were romping in and out of the water.

To save any argument, Terry quietly paid the small sum which enabled them to pass through, and, after pausing for a few moments to watch the swimmers, the three idly strolled towards the large, paved out-building dotted with small tables and chairs, at one end of which was a wide, curved counter.

Behind the counter, a large fair-haired girl was idly flicking a plate of rather weary-looking sandwiches.

As the three went up to the counter, she glanced across at them.

"We haven't any sandwiches yet, if that's what you want," she said. "These are only for show till we get the fresh ones in."

"We don't want sandwiches, thank you," said Julie, politely. "We were wondering if you had a message for us."

"Twins, aren't you?" said the girl. "Thought as much. You can't always tell, but I can. I've got a flair for that sort of thing—spotting things, you know. Sharp, my Ma calls me. Always have been. Many's the time she's said to me, Lucy, she's said, you want to watch out, my girl. You're so sharp one day you'll cut yourself. No, I haven't got no messages for nobody just at the moment."

"Oh—we thought——" began June.

"Mind jew," went on the girl, quite unperturbed. "We get a lot here—you'd be surprised. Girls leaving them for their boy friends and viccy versy."

"Viccy——?" began Julie in a puzzled tone.

"Vice versa," hissed Terry in her ear. "Free Latin."

"Telephone messages and all. You'd be surprised sometimes. Well, I have to laugh. They're not all written, you know. Many of them I have to give personal-like. You'd be surprised what some people consider a message, you would. But there it is. No, it's a bit early yet for that sort of thing. Better come back about midday or so, and I spect I'll be having something for you then. Boy friend, eh? I bet you share 'em out between you, being as you're both so alike. Sorry I can't oblige right away. I gotta go and make the cawfee. Be seein' you—better make it nearer one. Ta ta for now."

The blonde vanished, leaving the three a trifle breathless.

"Well—what now?" said June, after a moment.

"I can't face that woman for another single second," declared Julie, firmly. "Let's go outside somewhere and work it out."

"I entirely agree," added Terry. "Back to the Bug."

He firmly grasped the girls and fairly hurled them out of the place.

The man behind the pay-desk leant forward anxiously, but Terry beamed at him, shouted something to the effect that they'd left it in the car, and went flying down the steps, pulling the twins with him.

In a few moments, they were recovering their breath in the car, which was parked under a large tree.

"Short of returning at midday, or nearer one, when

she may be able to oblige, what do we do now?" asked Terry at last.

"We don't go back there," declared Julie, forcefully. "We've gone wrong somewhere, anyway. Mr. X would have left the clue there by now if we were supposed to get it from there."

"Or viccy versy," added June, her voice trembling with suppressed laughter.

"Free Latin," chorused Terry and Julie, and collapsed in another spasm of mirth.

"Oh dear, oh dear, we do 'ave fun," gasped Terry at last, retrieving a packet of very squashed cigarettes from his hip pocket and lighting one. "And now, my beloved 'earers, you'd better resurrect that there clue and try again, cos you've gorn wrong somewhere, that I know. You can't always tell, but I can. I've got a flair for spotting things like that."

"Oh, do be quiet!" begged Julie. "You sound like a rather messy feeder advertising a dry-cleaning shop."

"Oh, you rude child," exclaimed Terry. "Now I shan't let you use my soap."

The twins giggled, but their minds were on the difficult question of the missing clue.

"If anything had gone wrong, and Mr. X hadn't been able to get to the baths, there'd be no clue," said Julie, after a moment.

The girls glanced at Terry who shook his head violently.

"Don't look at me," he said. "I've got nothing to do with it, cross my heart, may I never see the back of my neck. Besides, if we'd managed to lay hands on Mr.

X the *Tribune* would have carried headlines this morning, the other papers would have had a special edition, and the broadcasting people would have seized up, as like as not."

"Not that we disbelieve you, but you're quite right, of course," said June.

"Sorry to be suspicious," added Julie, with a brilliant smile.

"Quite all right," said Terry. "I'd probably have done the same in your place. But, mind you, it doesn't have to be the police."

The girls looked at him inquiringly.

"Well, anything could have happened. He might have had a puncture, or the car broke down, or he overslept—he might even have sadly under-estimated your great brains, not realising that you had me to help you, and allowed a couple of days for you to solve the clue."

There were shrieks of protest from the twins, who declared in one voice that they knew they were brilliant, and that they needed no help whatsoever to solve any stupid little clue.

When order had once more been restored, they returned to the question of what to do next.

"I really can't face our friend, Viccy Versey, again," declared Terry. "If you must come back at nearer one, you do it by yourselves."

"I don't see any alternative, do you?" asked Julie.

"Yes, he does," cut in June. "Didn't you say just now that we'd better have another look at the clue because we'd gone wrong somewhere?"

"I believe I did give vent to that masterly under-statement," Terry admitted modestly. "It's one of these little things that I throw off occasionally—entirely unappreciated, of course. In fact, pearls before swine aren't in it, really."

"Are you by any chance referring to us?" demanded Julie, threateningly.

"If you hadn't so rudely interrupted, I was going to add—or incense before unbelievers," said Terry, severely. "And you can take your choice!"

"It's no good," said June, laughing. "You'll obviously not get the better of him. Let's get back to the clue."

"That's the idea," said Terry. "Returning to our muttons as the French so charmingly put it, the clue, the clue, you have mis-read the clue."

"I don't believe it, but we'll have a look," said Julie, and extracted the rather creased card from the pocket of her blue check skirt.

Once more the one fair and red two heads bent together as the three studied it carefully.

"We can't have gone wrong," declared June. "Unless the whole thing is a complete hoax."

"Oh, it couldn't be," said Julie. "I mean, there's no reason for it."

"That's no good," declared Terry. "For that matter, there's no reason for any of it."

"How do you mean?"

"There's not the faintest possible reason for Mr. X spending half his time writing clues for you, or for you indulging in this fantastic treasure hunt with an

unknown quarry and an equally unknown organiser.
There's no reason, for that matter, for me to spend my
hard-earned leisure, to say nothing of my days of toil,
helping you to solve the aforementioned clues, etc.,
etc. There's no reason for any of it, and it wouldn't
surprise me if I woke up soon and found that I'd had
cheese for supper last night and you were all a nightmare—I mean, dream."

"That's better," said June. "Nightmare is nearly as
bad as swine—and we're neither."

"Well, we don't look much like a dream, either, do
we?" giggled Julie.

Terry looked at the two girls, their red curls glinting
in the sunshine, their very charming faces lightly
dusted with freckles, their green eyes alight with
amusement. They were sitting demurely in the car,
June next to him, Julie leaning over from the back seat,
and their wide-skirted blue check frocks with the crisp
white collars and cuffs underlined the delightful
picture they made.

"Dreams," he said, solemnly. "And quite the nicest
dreams I've had for some time."

Julie clapped her hands.

"Now isn't that sweet of him," she said. "Consider-
ing how awkward we've been and how we've taken
up all your hard-earned leisure and your days of toil,
I think that's very handsome of you."

"Handsome is as handsome does," said Terry. "And
now, can we discontinue this mutual admiration
society and see about this 'ere clue. I'm sure you've got
it wrong somewhere."

"We can't have," wailed June. "It's perfectly clear—water—total immersion which means swimming—changing room where you comb your hair—and the clue at the refreshment counter. We can't be wrong."

"You must be wrong," insisted Terry. "I absolutely refuse to believe that Mr. X has slipped up. He's altogether far too efficient."

"Let's assume that Terry's right, and we have got the clue upside-down or something," said Julie.

She propped her elbows on her knees, her chin on her clenched fists and frowned ferociously in an effort of concentration as she stared at the handwriting on the card.

June tucked her legs comfortably under her, laid one brown arm along the back of the seat and leant against the leather cushion as she studied the clue with equal concentration.

Terry lit a cigarette, and, leaning back, blew smoke rings thoughtfully into the still air.

He had his own ideas about the clue, but, in spite of the fact that he earnestly hoped the twins would lead him to Mr. X, he was very concerned with playing fair with them as far as he could, and, to his mind, helping them with the clue was not playing fair.

So he sat back, smoking a cigarette and blowing smoke rings very successfully, while the girls stared at the clue and tried to see if they had gone wrong with it and where.

Presently, Terry threw away his cigarette and turned to look at them.

"No glimmer of light?" he inquired.

"I can't see that anything but swimming is meant," said June.

"It couldn't be anything but a swimming pool, surely," added Julie.

"I quite agree," said Terry.

The girls looked at him.

"I thought you said we'd read the clue wrong," protested Julie.

"I think you have," smiled Terry.

"Oh, don't be so infuriating," June burst out. "You say you agree that it couldn't be anything but the baths and yet we've got it wrong."

"Mis-quote," grinned Terry. "Your precise words were 'a swimming pool'."

"Well——?" began June.

Julie suddenly clapped a hand to her mouth and stared at him round-eyed.

"That's right," nodded Terry.

"What?" demanded June.

"We don't know that it's this swimming bath," said Julie. "We just jumped to the conclusion that it must be the Municipal baths, but, of course, there are dozens of others."

"But——" began June, and stared again at the clue.

"It doesn't say anything about it being here—the big baths," insisted Julie. "It could be Cranborne or Avondale or Hatfield or any of the outlying parts of the town where they've got a swimming pool."

"Well, for that matter, it could be a private one," said June, indignantly. "And hundreds and hundreds of people have swimming pools in their gardens."

"That's not so likely," said Terry, smiling lazily.

"I suppose not," she agreed. "But then—don't tell me we've got to rush round to all the suburbs which've got one and ask for a message?"

"It looks like it," grinned Terry. "That is, unless you can whittle it down a bit."

"What d'you mean—whittle it down?" asked Julie.

"Well—er—I can't believe Mr. X—with his consideration and forethought—would have set you a clue that put miles on the speedometer, consumed an enormous amount of petrol—expensive petrol—always provided you could use a car—and would undoubtedly over-develop your leg muscles if you had to cycle," explained Terry.

The girls looked at him.

"You know where it is, don't you," said Julie, accusingly.

Terry waved a hand.

"Let's say I've a hunch," he said. "Psychic, that's what I am. I'm very good at thought-reading, too," he added, severely.

The girls giggled.

"Your ears should be burning if you can read our thoughts at this moment," declared June.

"Look—never mind what you think of me. Time passes, and if you're going to get anywhere, just concentrate on that clue, will you?"

Obediently, the girls looked at the clue again.

June gave up after a few moments, and even Julie looked despondent.

"Just read it through and see if everything really

makes sense—really links up with the idea of Highlands Pool, say," Terry said, quite softly.

The girls looked at it again.

"I think so," frowned June. "The aqua plain—H_2O—total immersion——"

"Wait a minute," cut in Julie. "There's the bit about combing one's hair. I don't think that quite fits."

" Oh, yes," protested her sister. "You've got to comb your hair after you've been swimming."

"Some people don't," explained Julie. " And, anyway, the bit about not being considered vain doesn't really mean much, does it?"

"It's probably put in to rhyme."

Then June glanced at Terry and caught the expression on his face as he regarded them, a glint of amusement in his eyes.

"Is that it?" she asked.

"Could be," said Terry, quietly.

"Combing one's hair—not considered vain——" murmured Julie. "I still don't see what it ought to mean."

"What sort of people comb their hair," said Terry, helpfully.

"Why—everybody," answered June. "Everybody combs their hair some time or another."

"I see what you're getting at," put in Julie. "There's a cock's comb—that's the sort of thing you mean, isn't it?"

"You're certainly getting warmer," nodded the detective.

"Oh, I'm with you," declared June. "There's a curry-comb and a honeycomb and——"

"Hey, stick to the subject," protested Terry. "Combing—combing—people who comb."

"There's a lovely bit in *Taming of the Shrew* about 'To comb your noddle with a three-legged stool.' We did it last term, and it means beating you over the head with a milking stool," said Julie.

"Thanks very much. I said stick to the subject, remember?" said Terry, hastily.

"Well, it's a comb," said Julie.

"Wait a minute—I believe I've got it," said June.

"Well, don't keep it to yourself, darling," advised her sister.

"It's the vain part—not being vain to comb your hair. That's what it must be," explained June. "Somewhere or somebody and it's considered vain to comb her hair —that means she goes on combing it for a long time, doesn't she?"

"You remind me of the quiz people," grinned Terry. "They're not sure about the answer to a question, so they just go on talking round it for a few minutes and then they get a great light and all is crystal-clear."

"It's not crystal-clear to me," laughed June. "Anyway, we've got as far as somebody who combs her hair a lot——"

"Golden hair," exclaimed Julie.

"Why golden?" asked June. "It doesn't say that."

"I don't know," declared Julie, a trifle puzzled. "I don't even know why I said it. It just seemed to go, sort of thing. You know. Combing their golden hair."

"Who comb their golden hair?" asked Terry, softly.

"Mermaids, of course," chorused the twins.

" Don't you know?" added Julie. "They sit on the rocks, combing their golden hair and singing softly the songs that lure all poor sailors to their doom."

"That's right," agreed Terry and looked at the sisters.

There was a tiny pause.

Then the girls let out a screech and fell upon each other in an access of delight.

"Mermaids," they yodelled. "Mermaids—Mermaid's Pool—oh, panjandrums—oh, glory—oh, Mermaid's."

"That's right," said Terry.

"You might have told us," they reproached him.

"Uh-huh, not me," he said firmly. "It's your treasure hunt—your clues—your brain fag. Remember?"

"But it is Mermaid's, isn't it? Can we go there now?" asked Julie.

Terry nodded and settled back into the driving seat.

"Yes, ma'am," he said, and switched on the ignition.

"Thank you very much indeed," said Julie demurely, sitting back and tucking her long legs to one side more comfortably.

"It's a pleasure," declared Terry, and swung the small red car in the direction of Mermaid's Pool.

Out of the town, on to the double carriage-way of the broad Highlands road, through the suburb of beautiful houses and large gardens, past Governor's Lodge, where lived the Governor of Southern Rhodesia and his family, with African sentries, smartly uniformed on guard duty at the gates. Then the restricted area was ended, and on the broad tarred road Terry pressed the accelerator down and the speedometer crept up to 50—55—60, and there he held her, while fields and hedges slipped by, a native kraal flashed past, and the wind tugged at the girls' hair and blew their skirts.

Then they were off the tarred road, and slowing down to take the narrow side turning, raising a cloud of dust behind them.

The little car slid sideways on the fine grey sand as Terry swung her into the road that twisted and turned amongst enormous boulders and past thin, twisted msasa trees, till he braked for the big wooden barrier, and the round thatched rondavel that was used as a pay-box.

Terry handed the small African piccanin the correct entrance money and received three tickets torn from a big roll by the solemn youngster with the wide grin.

Once more he sent the car forward down a steep hill, round a bend, past some rondavels which were let through the season as holiday bungalows, and finally brought her to rest on the wide apron of grass which bordered Salisbury's weekend playground.

To one side were the tennis courts, flanked by the huge open-sided rondavel which served as a tea-room. At the other side was the refreshment counter with the kitchen behind it and, perched on the rocky hillside a little farther up, were the small changing rooms, while in front stretched the inviting expanse of the huge pool, sunlight flickering on the surface, the tall trees round the edge throwing a deep shade.

Where the stream fell into the pool down the hillside, the rocks had been smoothed away to make a wide, water-covered slide which was one of the main attractions, while from one side to the other, right across the pool, an aerial wire was strung, down which swimmers could come swinging to drop into the water.

"Mermaid's Pool," said June, softly.

"Where they comb their golden hair," added Julie.

"Not here they don't," declared Terry, climbing stiffly out of the car. "There's the refreshment counter, my hearties, and I'm extremely short of a little refreshment. What are we wasting time for?"

In a state of high excitement, the two girls walked across to the small counter, with Terry by their side.

The woman behind the counter, was the fat, jolly type, with a round, red face and a broad smile.

As the twins asked whether she had a message for them, she looked at them and laughed.

"Twins is reet," she said, in broad Yorkshire. "It's plain t'see. A message? Aye, I've a message for t'twins, reet enow. Ee, I mun 'ave it somewheer."

She hunted through the pocket of her capacious apron, and finally discovered it tucked into the calendar hanging on the wall.

"Here y'are, luv," she said, handing over the familiar white envelope.

With murmured thanks, the little group turned away.

"It's the same envelope," said Julie. "It's from Mr. X all right."

"It's the next clue," agreed June. "Isn't this exciting."

"I do hope it's not going to be frantically difficult to solve," added Julie.

"Perhaps I can help you solve it," said a voice behind them, and they spun round to stare at the dark, rather untidy-looking young man, with the crumpled shirt, faded tie and ancient corduroy trousers, who stood smiling at them, a camera in his hand.

CHAPTER VI

A LEARNED CLUE

THERE WAS a long moment of silence while the girls stared at the young man, and the young man laughed back at them.

Then Terry stretched out a hand and clapped him on the shoulder.

"Don!" he said. "Don Rawlings! What in all the world are you doing here?"

"You'd be surprised," was the reply.

"Don't tell me there's been a murder and you're photographing the scene of the crime. Anyway, you're a reporter, not a camera man, surely?"

"Normally, yes, but in moments of great strain, when the resources of the entire South African News Agency are strained to breaking point, who rushes into the breach regardless of personal comfort, trade union rules, or petty considerations of that kind?"

"Don Rawlings?" inquired Terry.

"Well, actually, it's usually the boss, but on this occasion the office boy's got the job," grinned Don. "So I'm here—me in person, as Dickens so concisely puts it."

"Really? What for?" asked Terry. "Oh, by the way," he added quickly, "let me introduce you all. This is Don Rawlings, considered to be the world's greatest reporter, by himself, at the moment apprenticed to S.A.N.A.—mainly because they weren't looking at that exact moment. Don, this is June and this is Julie Kennedy."

The girls smiled at the irrepressible young man, and Don made them an elaborate bow.

"The next question, of course, is: 'Twins, I presume?'," he said. "But I'm not that sort. I never ask or do the expected. And, anyway, a blind man with lumbago could see you were twins. What I want to know instead is—why June and Julie?"

"Why not?" asked June.

"Well, it doesn't seem to match up, somehow," explained the ridiculous creature. "I mean, twins—June and Julie. Why not April and May? Or Christmas and New Year?"

"Those aren't girls' names," said Julie.

"My dear June—or is it Julie? Anyway, my dear Jay, I'd have you know that there is now living in England a child who was christened Merry."

"Merry?" chorused the twins.

"Her father's name is Day," explained Don, solemnly. "What's more, I have personally made the acquaintance of a young lady who has for years suffered under the handicap of two Christian names—Easter and Daffodil. She was given those by enthusiastic parents for the obvious reason that she happened to be born in a year when Easter was on a Sunday and she appeared just then."

"Same with us," said Julie, suddenly.

"I beg your pardon?"

"I said, same with us," repeated Julie. "Hence June and Julie."

Terry started to laugh as the young man stared at the girls with something like horror.

"J-J-June and Julie?" he inquired.

"That's right. Same as April and May. My sister was born in June—I was born in July," explained Julie, solemnly.

Don ran a hand through his thick, dark hair and stared at the girls with a rather dazed expression.

"Terry, old man," he said at last. "Remind me to buy a dictionary when we get back to town, will you? I want to look up the definition of twins."

"Oh, we're twins all right," explained June. "But I'm the eldest."

"The—eldest—twin?" stammered Don.

"That's right. We're quite unique, you know. We have a birthday each—two birthdays on different days."

"What I need is a lot of strong drink," said Don, wildly. "My nerve's going—I'm hearing things—I think I'm seeing things, too."

"She's quite right," giggled Julie. "June was born on 30th June at about 11.30 p.m. I was born on 1st July at about 1 a.m. You can work it out from there."

It was five minutes and a cup of strong coffee before Don had recovered sufficiently to realise that the four of them were sitting round one of the check-covered tables in the big refreshment rondavel, with Terry drinking coffee opposite him, and the two red heads with the attractive green eyes and freckles, sitting between them, solemnly eating their way through huge slices of home-made cream cake washed down with bottles of orange fizzy drinks sucked very satisfactorily through straws.

Then his wandering glance took in the square white envelope which was lying by the side of June—or was it Julie's plate?

They were arguing amicably about the possibilities of having a swim.

"I've got a towel and a pair of swimming trunks in the car," said Terry, with a smirk. "But you two haven't got any swimsuits, have you?"

"We can manage," said June, firmly.

"How?" demanded Terry.

"There's May Fenton over there," explained Julie. "She'll lend us a swimsuit—she never has less than two with her, 'cos she likes to change into a dry one as soon as she's been swimming."

"But you can't both get into one," protested Terry.

"Oh, no, but Mrs. Mac, up at the house, has ones she often lends us," added June. "Don't worry—we're quite good at getting organised on occasions like this."

"In that case, we'll all swim," declared Terry.

"What?" yelled Don, suddenly realising what everybody was saying. "Swim? At this time of year? In this temperature?"

"It's not very cold," said June, in surprise. "It was something like 60 at the town baths yesterday according to the board they have in the entrance hall."

"But this is *not* the town baths—this is a natural river—and it's pure snow-broth at present," declared Don.

The twins looked at each other and smiled.

Then Julie turned to Terry.

"Shall I borrow a pair of trunks from Mrs. Mac, too?" she asked, demurely. "She's always got a few spares."

Terry grinned broadly.

"You do that small thing," he said. "And I'll take care of the rest."

The twins hurriedly finished their drinks and set off to climb the small hill, at the top of which was a single-story white house set in a garden full of flowers, even at this time of the year.

Five minutes later they were back, with June swinging a vivid yellow and black satin swimsuit from one hand, and carrying a couple of towels in the other, while Julie flourished a pair of blue trunks and a third towel.

"Here you are," she said, tossing them across to Terry. "I'm going to collect a suit from May."

"Five minutes and we'll see you in the pool," nodded Terry, and led the still protesting Don off towards the changing rooms.

It was rather less than five minutes when the two girls, June in the yellow and black suit, and Julie in a striking affair of scarlet and white, came running down the stone steps, flung their towels on the grass and dived into the pool.

Half a minute later, Terry joined them, and the three

raced across to the opposite side, pulled themselves out of the water, and went running across to mount the tall ladder and come sliding down on the aerial way to drop into the water again near the centre.

As they swam towards the shore, they saw the shivering figure of the young reporter standing on the bank.

"What's it like?" he called to them.

"Wonderful," they cried. "Come on in."

"Is it cold?"

"Freezing," they yelled.

Don moaned gently, and stepped back. But before he could do anything, Terry, close to the bank, scrambled out, ran up to him, gave him a well-timed push and sent him flying in to the water.

"Can he swim?" asked Julie, a trifle anxiously.

"Like a fish," laughed Terry. "He's only putting it on. He's all right, really."

"Who is he, actually?" asked June.

" A reporter on the staff of the South African News Agency. He's inclined to bound a little, but, as long as you're firm with him, he's bearable."

"But what's he doing here?" asked Julie. " Does he know anything about the clues?"

"I shouldn't have thought so, though he knows all about Mr. X, of course, and the McIlwaine business," said Terry, thoughtfully.

"I thought he knew about the clues by the way he came up behind us and offered to help," declared June.

"Ye-es. Could be. Anyway, we'll drag it out of him

in a few minutes. Leave it to me," said Terry, and the three went racing over to Don.

Terry was right, thought June. Don could swim like any fish. In fact, he made rings round them all, though the twins were considered first-class swimmers and Terry was no mean performer himself.

His dives were spectacular, his crawl was the fastest thing they'd seen, and his butterfly stroke was a joy to watch and impossible to imitate.

"Where on earth did you learn to swim?" asked Julie, as they finally got out and sat on the bank, towelling themselves.

"Didn't you know?" said Don. "My papa was a wizard, and he made a spell when I was born to make sure that I would have not only beauty but b-brains as well. But something went wrong with the spell and, instead of growing brains, I grew fins. Mother was simply furious, of course, and they had a first-class row about it. However, they made it up when Papa's familiar, a huge black cat called Othello, knocked me backwards into the swimming pool, and, instead of drowning I swam happily three times round the pool and they had to get me out with a fishing net. After that, I appeared all over England as the Fish Prodigy and Mother simply roped in the shekels and was delighted, of course."

"You are a clown," said Terry, calmly, while the twins rocked with laughter.

"Not clown, dear heart, just The Swimming Wonder," explained Don. "Of course, it didn't last. I grew too big and the fins too small, so Papa made another spell and got rid of them altogether. Mother was a bit acid, but it wasn't any good. Papa tried the first spell again, and overdid it, and a small cousin of ours turned into a real fish."

"What happened to him?" asked Julie.

"We really never knew. It was on a Friday, so we rather think he was fried and eaten for supper by the housekeeper. Anyway, it put an end to Papa's spells with fishes. Let's go and imbibe some strong, hot beverage. I feel like Hilary at the South Pole."

Don got to his feet, and led the way to the refreshment place, where he amazed the African waiter by ordering four, double-strength, double-size and twice-as-hot coffees.

With towels to sit on, and the strong African sun pouring in, they were all quite warm within a few minutes, and they were soon having a second meal of coffee and cake.

" And now shall we unburden ourselves to each other, or go on indulging in Polite Conversation and Party Manners?" asked Terry.

"I'm all for unburdening," said Julie, and June nodded agreement.

"Not that I'm in any way a camel or similar b-b-beast of b-b-burden," agreed Don. "But I do so see what you mean. Who'll start?"

"You," chorused the three.

Don looked slightly startled, but Terry went on firmly.

"Firstly, what're you doing here, and don't say having yourself a ball or other repulsive expressions, because I know that look in your eye when you're on the job," he said. "And that look's right in your eye now."

"All right, I won't," said Don, obligingly.

"And secondly why should you think you can help us with a clue," added June.

"Alas, alas, all is undone," said Don, sadly. "I see that I must confess all."

"That's right," agreed the three.

"In that case, the answer is that I'm on a job, I'm here for the purpose, and I'm terribly, terribly keen on puzzles," he said, earnestly.

"That's no answer, Don," declared Terry. "What's your job here?"

"We-ell——" began Don.

"It's to do with us, isn't it?" said Julie, brutally.

"Yes, it is," said Don, frankly.

"Go on," urged Terry. "How did you work that one?"

"For that matter, how did you?" asked Don. "And why are you in on it?"

There was a short pause.

"Do we put all our cards on the table?" asked Terry.

"You can play snap with them—I don't mind," said Don. "It's up to you."

They both looked at the twins.

"I think we might just as well all know where we stand," said June, after a moment.

"You start, then, brother," said Don.

"That's easy. I'm stringing along with the twins because they are at the moment our only link with

Mr. X," explained Terry, rapidly. "It's all strictly unofficial, of course, but we do know and they admit that they're playing this fantastic game with our unknown friend, and so the powers-that-be thought it as well if we could keep tabs on them."

"So now you're their dearest friend," said Don, brutally.

"He's quite nice," said Julie. "But I think it's only fair to tell you that we are not going to give Mr. X away. We explained that to Terry. We just couldn't sort of help Mr. X to get arrested, even though we don't know him. We sorted it out with Terry, and he's promised to let us know before he does anything drastic, so that we can warn Mr. X—we're not very happy about it, but there it is."

"So I understand," said Don, gravely.

The twins looked at him.

"It's not very satisfactory all round," explained Terry. "But we haven't a single lead at the moment, as you probably know."

"I do indeed," grinned Don. "So you think the twins might give you one—and then you can step in quickly and collect Mr. X before they've time to warn him?"

"That's the idea," nodded Terry.

"Brother, you will have to get up a lot earlier," advised Don.

"Maybe. We'll skip that for the moment. Where do you come in on this?"

" On the same lines as you, except that I don't want to arrest him," said Don.

"Then—what are you doing here?" asked June.

"We're in much the same position as the police," he explained. "We're not a bit interested in arresting him, but we're more than anxious to get a story and pictures. South Africa, which is our head office, is fairly squealing for them. Like the police, we've not the faintest clue of where or what or who he is. So, if I may string along with you—you being our only possible lead at the moment."

The twins looked at each other.

"I—well, we seem to be very popular," said Julie, with a small laugh.

"I assure you, you are. In fact, it surprises me that you can move hand or foot without all the local reporters and camera men round you," nodded Don.

"Just a minute—how come you got on to this?" asked Terry, looking hard at Don.

"Oh, you know me," said Don, lightly. "Always the little Sherlock Holmes. My maternal grandmother was a bloodhound, actually, and I've inherited many of her tendencies. I can uncover a clue with the best of them. Like you, I'm more or less unofficially on leave—the boss only wants me to return with a notebook full of details and a camera full of pix of Mr. X, and I shall be the white-headed boy. So my immediate ambition was to get alongside the twins."

"That's no explanation," said Terry. "How did you know about them—and that they would be here this morning?"

"I have my spies everywhere," said Don, loftily.

"You see that little bird over there, so innocently looking at us?"

He pointed to a small brown bird perched on the nearby rail, head on one side, bright eyes darting here and there.

"Well, he's not one of them," went on Don. "But his fourth cousin twice removed is on the pay-roll."

"Quit stalling, Don," said Terry, and there was a hard note in his voice which the girls had not heard before. "How did you turn up here?"

"All right—all right—I give in," said Don.

He turned to the girls.

"Sorry—I tried to stall—but he'll get to know in the end," he said.

The girls stared at him, round-eyed with surprise.

"I told you you'd have to get up a good deal earlier to get ahead of these two, Terry," he went on. "And you never read your morning paper to-day, did you? I recommend the Personal Column."

He tossed a folded copy of the *Tribune* across to Terry, sat back and lit a cigarette.

The girls looked at each other a little nervously, while Terry riffled through the pages until he came to the one with the Personal Column printed on it. He read it through quickly and then folded up the paper and slowly handed it back to Don.

"We're sorry about that," said Julie. "But honestly we felt it was only fair to warn him, and we'd no idea how to get in touch with him. We didn't like to put his name or ours, so we just put in the clue."

"And I suppose you recognised the style of verse,

same as I did with the previous clue," said Terry, and Don nodded.

"It didn't take long to work it out that it was Mermaids, and anyway it was sufficiently interesting to take a run out here and see just who was making pretty rhymes about it. When I saw you here, I knew you were on the same trail—since you've always been on the Mr. X case—and it was obvious you weren't just frittering your time away with these youngsters. Therefore, the twins must be your lead," added Don. "So here we all are."

Terry threw his cigarette away and drained his coffee cup.

"All right," he said. "Where do we go from here?"

"Doesn't that make any difference?" asked Julie, pointing to the paper. Terry shrugged his shoulders and smiled.

"Not from my point of view. I still think I'll beat you all. It makes no difference whether you warn Mr. X—sooner or later I'll pick him up all right."

"Fair enough," said June. "And I'm sorry we felt we had to do it."

"Think nothing of it. I'm really quite sympathetic," said Terry. "And now let's get ahead with the next clue, shall we?"

"What about me?" asked Don. "Can we make it a foursome?"

"We don't mind," said Julie, and looked inquiringly at Terry.

"I'm used to him. He won't get in my hair," said Terry.

"I'm really quite harmless," went on Don. "And I only want a story from him and some pictures when we finally contact your Mr. X. If you let me have them, you'll find life much easier. Otherwise, you'll have half a dozen reporters all panting at your heels— pictures of you both in every paper—probably the newsreel men, too, and the Federal Broadcasting crowd."

The twins stared at him in horror.

"But why?" they asked.

"Because as soon as you get anywhere near Mr. X you're going to be News with a capital N," explained Don. "Even now, if the *Tribune* men got a sniff of this, they'd be on to you."

"But we don't know that we're ever going to get near Mr. X," protested June. "We may never even see him at all."

"We'll take a chance on that," grinned the reporter. "Can't you see the headlines? Charming Twins Play Treasure Hunt with Mr. X. Mysterious Burglar Lays Trail for Twins. Pictures on page 3."

The two girls went pale at the very thought.

"What on earth would Father say?" exclaimed June.

"Mother would have a seizure," added Julie.

"We never thought of anything like that," they chorused.

"Better think of it now," advised Don.

"He's quite right," said Terry. "If this story breaks, you'll be front page news all over Southern Africa."

"Well, it mustn't," declared June, in considerable agitation.

"Take it easy," said Terry, soothingly. "I'm on your side—it wouldn't suit us in the least. And Don's quite reliable in this matter. He'll try and fend off everybody else for as long as possible."

"You bet I will," cut in Don, fervently. "This story is going to put me right at the top, if I can keep the vultures off it."

"But another little caper like this, and you may well find the whole thing blown wide-open," added Terry, jabbing at the newspaper. "Just remember that I got on to you two through that second printed clue, and now Don's picked you up after this one. Goodness knows how many others will have had their brains working the same way."

The twins stared round nervously.

"C-could we go?" asked Julie. "I mean, we've got the next clue—we needn't waste time here, need we?"

"If we're not here, nobody can—er—pick us up, can they?" added June.

"Right," nodded Terry. "Five minutes to change, and we'll foregather at the Bug."

"Me, too?" inquired Don.

The twins smiled and nodded.

"Why not?" said June. "According to Terry, you're going to be our salvation."

"I've never been a salvation before," said Don, solemnly. "I think I'll be very good in the part."

"Is your car here?" asked Terry, and Don nodded. "Then I suggest you follow us back to town," he went on. "We've obviously got to stand by while the twins solve the next clue, so we'd better go somewhere quiet and out-of-the-way, where neither you nor I are likely to be recognised."

"How right you are," said Don. "Anybody seeing us in cahoots will immediately smell fifteen enormous rats."

"Let's go home, then," suggested June. "We can sit in the garden and work on the clue, and at least it's quiet and comfortable."

"What could be better?" asked Don. "Five minutes from now."

The twins fled to the changing room, and, in five and a quarter minutes, a trifle breathless and with damp curls, but otherwise quite in one piece, as June put it, they climbed into the Bug, and Terry started the engine.

Behind them Don got into his small car and followed them as they drove away from Mermaid's Pool.

Half an hour later both cars swung into the drive and the four got out and walked across the lawn.

With the usual shrieks of joy, the Dachshunds came rushing out to greet them. Terry they also greeted, and, although they were a trifle wary of Don, and carefully sniffed round him, they decided to accept him also as a friend, and the four were soon sitting on the stoep, while Julius produced coffee and cool drinks, and June opened the envelope containing the next clue.

Two red heads, one fair and the fourth dark bent over the now familiar square of white card and studied the writing.

" *This next clue you will find quite tame where the greatest*

*queen is only a name. The one you want is full of signs, of
particles and also lines. The name should not be too hard to
find for it's particles of all mankind.*"

There was a moment's silence after June read it out.
Then everybody sat back and said "Phew!" in heart-
felt tones.

"I think you'll have to help us with this," said Julie,
looking at the two men.

"Help!" said Don. "It's no use expecting me to
translate that. I'm better at engineering. My paternal
parent was a great one with his hands. In fact, it was
due to him that the family motto was changed to
' Fingers Before Forks '. My grandmother was simply
furious about it."

"What was your family motto before that?" asked
June, her eyes dancing.

"Rather nice, really," said Don. "Cry, baby, cry.
Put your finger in your eye."

"Well, it's b-b-brains before b-b-brawn that we want
now," said Terry, brutally.

"Oh, but how harsh!" exclaimed Don. "And,
anyway, don't let's waste any more time in idle chatter.
To work, to work—as the Labour officer said to
somebody."

"Do you really want us to help you?" asked Terry.

"There's no reason why you shouldn't," said Julie.
"I mean, Mr. X didn't suggest that only we were to
solve the clues."

"And, if it's a question of time, we could do with a
little help," added June.

"It's certainly a question of time before the *Tribune*

boys wake up to the fact that you're playing clues with Mr. X," said Don. "To say nothing of the Sunday papers and the rest."

The twins shuddered and June pushed the clue towards him.

"Come on, then. Let's get down to it," said Terry, briskly.

In a few moments, they all had paper and pencils and were hard at work.

"Let's list the items first," suggested Julie. "There's a queen, signs, particles and lines."

"Don't forget mankind," said Terry. "Most important."

"Or a red herring," said June.

The four studied the list Julie had made.

"Clear as mud, isn't it," murmured Terry.

"I don't think there's much of a pun anywhere, like there was in the last two," said June. "Perhaps that's why he says it's tame."

"Tame!" snorted Don. "I'd hate to see a clue he considered wild."

"Let's start at the beginning," suggested Terry. "First of all, the queen—the greatest queen."

"Who's the greatest queen?" asked June.

"There's plenty of queens to choose from," declared Don. "There's Queen Anne and her bounty, which still exists and is money used to supplement the miserable incomes most padres get from the parishes. Then there's the Queen of Hearts, which, believe it or not, is not only a playing card, but also a name for Elizabeth, Queen of Bohemia, poor lass."

"There's lots of queens," agreed Julie. "Like the Queen of the North and the Queen of Heaven."

"Saints defend us, don't let it be the Queen of the North," exclaimed Terry. "That's Edinburgh and nothing would induce me to go half across the world to Edinburgh for the next clue."

"I should think the Queen of Heaven would be the greatest queen," said Julie.

"That covers a wide field," said Don. "A lot of religions go in for a Queen of Heaven—the Phoenicians, the Greeks, the Romans, the——"

"Stop!" cried the twins.

"Sorry," said Don, eyebrows raised. "I'm a bit of an expert on queens. My great-grandmother was——"

"*Not* a qu-eee-een?" said Julie, in mock astonishment.

"Certainly not," replied Don, severely. "She was a weather prophet, and when the Queen—that was Queen Victoria at that time—announced that she intended to pay a visit to Whortleberry-on-the-Wimbush the local inhabitants asked my great-grandmother which was the best day for sun. They didn't want rain, you see, because it ruined the Vicar's temper and washed the dye out of all the flags. So she told them which day would be summer that year, with the sun shining, and they settled for it, and she was quite right. The sun shone all day, and it was so hot that even the dairymaids melted in the dairy, and simply ran everywhere. And Queen Victoria was delighted, and ever after that, it's called Queen's Weather when it doesn't rain at a bazaar or a fete."

"Queen Victoria!" said June, eyes round with surprise. "She was one of the greatest queens, wasn't she?"

"Of course," chorused the others. "Queen Victoria!"

"It's no good—the old lady died some years ago, and I refuse to believe the next clue is on her tomb in England—Windsor, I think," said Terry.

"But isn't there a statue of her in Salisbury?" asked Julie. "I'm sure I've seen one somewhere."

"Not a statue—the library," said June. "The Queen Victoria Memorial Library. D'you think there could be a clue there?"

"Almost certainly," said Don, with a hideous laugh. "It's hidden in a book, and you've got to guess which of the five thousand, four hundred and thirty two and a half books is hiding it. You get one point for everyone with over seventeen hundred pages, and cobwebs count half a point extra."

"Don't be ridiculous," laughed Julie. "Anyway, let's get on with the clue. What about these particles?"

"Just a minute, though," said Terry, slowly. "Why shouldn't it be in the library?"

"What—with five thousand and what'sit books there?" asked June, in surprise.

"Well, the rest of the clue might help us there," he explained. "It's worth thinking about, anyway. Suppose it's a book—where does that get us?"

"On friendly terms with a bookworm if we've any sense," declared Don. "My cousin was very friendly with one, but it didn't do him any good. He merely learnt to chew his way through books instead of reading them."

"Oh, do be quiet!" exclaimed June, in some exasperation.

"Sorry—I thought I was being helpful," replied Don, in hurt tones. "You know, the little ray of sunshine."

"Anything less like a ray of sunshine——" began Terry.

"Well, if you'd rather I appeared in a yellow ballet frock and danced here and there, I'm willing to oblige. I mean, I'll try anything once."

"Be quiet," said everybody, very loudly, and Don subsided into a hurt silence.

"Suppose Terry's right, and it is a book, where does that get us with signs and particles?" asked Julie.

Don opened his mouth, but received such an awful look from the twins that he closed it again.

"I suppose there wouldn't be a book on particles, would there?" asked June.

"I've never heard of one," confessed Terry.

"Signs?" asked Julie.

"Zodiac," whispered Don, very softly. "Signs of the Zodiac."

The others looked at him.

"A book about stars?" asked June, thoughtfully. "Stars in their Courses or something like that?"

"Sounds very Huxley to me," laughed Terry. "Let's try a bit further."

"There isn't any further," said Julie. "It's all signs and particles and lines and particles."

"Gently, gently," said Terry. "The one we want

looks as though it might be a book—a book full of signs——"

"That could be printing and figures," suggested Julie.

"Could be," agreed Terry. "Also of particles and lines—lines in a book all right."

"And the name should not be hard to find," read June. "That could be the title of the book—I think you're right. It is a book."

"The name—the name is particles of all mankind," said Julie, staring at the clue. "What on earth can that mean? What's particles?"

"Got a dictionary?" asked Don. "Particles is little bits of things but the dictionary meaning might help."

Julie ran indoors to fetch a dictionary and came out with the big book open at the right page.

"Doesn't help much," she said. "Listen. Particle—minute portion of matter, smallest possible amount, atom, minor part of speech—etc., etc., and all sorts of bits and pieces after it."

Don and Terry looked at each other and laughed. Then they both stood up.

"Well, there we are, my beloved 'earers," said Terry. "Next stop—the library. Come on, twins."

The girls stared at him open-mouthed.

"D'you mean—you've solved it?" gasped Julie.

"'S'right," nodded Don. "Always place your trust in dictionaries—books dealing with alphabets—word-books—lexicons—let's go."

"But what—who—which——" clamoured the girls.

"What book—what's the name?" demanded Julie. Terry stopped and looked at them in some surprise.

"Why—aren't you with us?" he asked. "*Atoms of Man*—well-known reference book used by all the best people and to be found in every library worthy of the name. Come on, folks."

CHAPTER VII

HOW RED IS A HERRING !

THIS TIME all four piled into the M.G. for, as Don said, although it was a bit of a lemon squash it wasn't for long, and it saved him petrol.

It was only a few minutes along the avenues to the library, and Terry was soon parking the car at one side of the big, old-fashioned red brick building that housed not only the library but also the museum.

The twins had on one or two occasions been to the museum with the school, and found the exhibits quite delightful—the animals of Rhodesia beautifully stuffed and placed in glass cases, and many other interesting things—but, on this occasion, they ignored the flight of steps that led up to the museum and went straight through into the library itself.

They paused for a moment to stare in bewilderment at the thickly packed shelves that lined the different rooms from floor to as high as one could reach.

"Where on earth do we find it?" asked June, in a whisper.

"Catalogue," said Terry, and steered her towards one corner where stood a filing cabinet of small drawers, each one filled with index cards and labelled alphabetically on the front.

"Who wrote it?" asked Julie.

"Don't be absurd," said Don, loudly. "Nobody wrote it—nobody could possibly write a thing like that—it just grew."

"Hush!" said the twins, a little overawed at the solemnity of the library.

They had been to the library before, but always at times when there were a great many people all changing books and strolling round.

It was obviously just before the luncheon rush, thought Julie, with everybody still working, and hardly anybody to be seen.

"Catalogue of subjects," said Terry, quietly, and in a moment had pulled out the right drawer, and was thumbing through the cards. "Here we are," he went on. "Atoms of Man—ten forty seven dash eight."

"That's a great help," said Julie. "Where do we go from here?"

"We ask," said Don. "If you think I'm going to spend the next three hours running up and down those shelves, peering at each book, you're wrong. And there's a nice, knowledgeable-looking lass just waiting to answer all our questions."

The others turned to look at the efficient, pleasant-looking librarian who was sorting through a pile of books.

By common consent, Terry went forward, and asked where they would find the book they were looking for.

"Oh, will you come through and I'll show you," she said, with a smile, and led them through a big archway into another room also lined with shelves.

"Just up there—where that gentleman is standing," she said, pointing to the far end of the room.

They thanked her and moved up the room together. Julie said something in a low voice, and Don laughed.

At the sound, the short, be-spectacled man at the far end of the room turned round to stare at them.

Then he hurriedly pushed the book he had in his hands back on to the shelf, dodged round a tall set of shelves that stood in the middle of the room, and disappeared quickly through the archway.

Don turned to stare at him.

"Gentleman in a hurry," he observed. "Perhaps we frightened him."

"One look——" began Terry, but stopped as Julie gave a cry of surprise.

"Isn't that amazing," she said. "That man must have been looking at the very book we want. Look— he's only just put it back, see? It's still half-out of the line."

She pulled it out and flicked through it. Her fingers encountered a stiff envelope, and she pulled it out.

Don and Terry were staring at each other.

"Mr. X," she said, softly.

"Come on," yelled Don, suddenly.

Grabbing the twins by the arm, they raced down the long room and through the archway, with Terry well ahead.

Out of the library they shot, to pause on the steps for a moment to stare round.

"There he is," shrieked Julie. "Look—that dark green car."

The others caught a glimpse of the dark-suited man driving out of the gates in a small, green Hillman of moderate age.

Without another word, the four raced across the gravel to the spot where Terry had parked the red M.G. and in a moment they were climbing in, while Terry was already moving off. Don, indeed, had to take a flying leap and landed in a heap of tangled arms and legs on the hood of the little car.

Then the M.G. was out of the gates. She was held up for what seemed like five minutes but was really only a few seconds, while the passing traffic went on its way.

Then there was a break, and the little car shot into the gap. The green Hillman was almost out of sight down the road, but Don, by this time standing up in the back, roared out instructions to Terry.

"He's passing the roundabout—no, he's turning right—he's going straight up the avenue—he's out of sight! Terry, for goodness sake, step on it, laddie!"

Terry obediently stepped on it, the car shot forward again, and Don collapsed once more, uttering loud 'tallyho' and other hunting noises to the infinite amusement of the group of Africans who giggled and grinned as the car went past them.

"Up the avenue—where on earth is he going?" asked Julie.

"Couldn't tell you," muttered Terry. "But we'll tail him and see."

"Can you see him yet?" asked June, craning her neck.

"I think—yes—yes, I've got him. Just going up to the crossroads at the top," said Julie.

"Try and watch him and see which way he turns," said Terry, endeavouring to pass a high, lumbering lorry.

He did so, scraping between the lorry and an oncoming Chevrolet of substantial size.

"He's—he's turning—he's turning right," said Julie. "He's out of sight again now."

"Good," said Terry. "We don't want to keep too close to him. Might scare him off."

As they came to the cross-roads, Terry turned right. There was plenty of traffic about, and his only worry at the moment was to make certain the quarry was not lost.

"Watch out for the traffic lights," he said, as he skimmed past two cars and settled down behind a large, black saloon.

The lights were evidently turning to green as the Hillman came up to them.

"Left," chorused the twins.

The Hillman shot ahead down the wide road, and Terry scraped round the corner, with the amber already turning to red.

There was now only one car between him and the Hillman, and again he settled down behind it, since it gave him reasonable cover, and yet enabled the four to watch the Hillman without being too obvious about it.

"I can't imagine where he's going," said Julie.

"Probably to Bulawayo," observed Don from the

back. "Tell me, Gunga Din, do we follow him that far?"

"Not if I can help it," said Terry. "I've more respect for the age and condition of this mousetrap."

"Brother, I am with you," agreed Don, feelingly. "I also have more respect for my anatomy than to wish to undertake several hundred soul-searing miles in the Bug. Besides, I hate being so near the ground."

"Look out, he's turning again—he's heading for the showground, isn't he?" said June.

"Looks like it," declared Julie. "What on earth goes on at the showground just now?"

"Nothing," declared Don, who, as a reporter, always knew what was happening at almost any place in Salisbury. "They're just clearing up after the show, and the entire place will sink into solitary silence, except for the occasional dog show until next year."

"Then what does Mr. X want to go there for?"

"Probably that's where he keeps his ill-gotten gains," suggested June.

"What, in the tobacco warehouse, or among the poultry cages?" asked Don.

"After all, we don't know that it *is* Mr. X," added Julie. "We only——"

"It's not the showground," cut in Don. "He's going straight past it."

"But this car ahead is going into the showground," added Julie.

"He *would* be," murmured June. "Why on earth couldn't he stay between us."

"What on earth do we do now?" asked Julie.

"Drop back a good bit and hope for the best," said Terry, slowing down as the car in front turned through the gates and went sailing down the main road in the showground.

The green Hillman was nearly out of sight before Terry picked up speed again, and then he was content to stay well behind.

The road was very wide, and carried the main Salisbury-Bulawayo traffic, as well as the numerous vehicles whose destinations were the intermediate towns of the busy Rhodesian Midlands.

It curved slightly to left and then to right, but on the whole it ran fairly straight, and although there was a certain amount of traffic, it was of the heavy lorry category which, of necessity, travelled very much more slowly than the Hillman or the M.G.

The Hillman forged steadily ahead, overtaking lorry after lorry, and the M.G. followed equally steadily, keeping always as far as possible from the green car ahead.

"I thought you said we wouldn't go to Bulawayo to-day," remarked Don, plaintively.

"Quite right," nodded Terry. "Hartley's the first town we come to, and there we stop, while I climb on the telephone. Salisbury can notify everybody down the road, and the Hillman will be watched all the way."

"What a blessing a telephone can be," said Don. "Hartley is just about as far as I can bear."

"I can't see why he should go to Bulawayo," said June. "Unless this clue is the last and that's the end of the story."

"In which case, he's moving out of town," said Terry.

"That's right," nodded Don. "And Bulawayo's conveniently near the border. If you're right, it's through Beit Bridge and into the Union for that lad to-morrow morning."

"I wonder," murmured Terry. "He can't have much stuff with him in that small car."

"Not so small," corrected Don. "And since when has jewellery taken up much room?"

"Jewellery, maybe, but not much family silver. And, anyhow, how the deuce is he going to get it through the customs at Beit Bridge?" demanded Terry.

"Probably as traveller's samples," said Don, with a grin.

"We don't know that he is leaving the country," protested June. "He may not even be going to Bulawayo."

"No, of course not," agreed Don. "He's probably an electrician on his way to a job at the Umniati Power Station. I remember my grandfather saying how extremely useful it was to be able to mend a fuse. And he was quite right, too. Only an hour or two later, a fuse blew, and Grandfather mended it beautifully. He hadn't any fuse wire, but he used one of Grandmother's little wire hairpins, and we had light in a matter of minutes."

"Was it all right?" asked Terry.

"Oh, most successful," said Don. "The fire engine managed to put out the fire after it had burned down the West wing, but the rest of the place was saved. And we didn't really mind about the West wing, you know. We hardly ever used it, and actually the only people it upset were the mice who lived on the tapestries, and the nun who was walled up there in the fifteenth century and had haunted it ever since."

"Poor thing," said Julie. "What a shame. And now she's homeless?"

"Well, actually, the Cavalier's ghost took pity on her, we fancy, and gave her——Look out, he's turning," he added, with a shout.

Sure enough, the green Hillman in the distance was disappearing down a turning on the right.

"That's the Norton turn-off," said Terry. "Norton —so that's where he's going. What on earth for?"

"If you travel at this speed much farther, we shall never know," said Don, eyes shut, as the M.G.'s speedo-meter needle went round the dial with a rush. "Not unless we inquire at the pearly gates."

"Sorry," said Terry, adding another five miles per hour to the speed.

As they drew level with the turning, he spun the wheel, and the car went skidding across the main road and along the Norton road.

"Could we go back, please?" said Don, in a small voice. "I left my lower stomach somewhere by that corner. Oh, and why did we have to pass a cemetery— I never knew there was one round here?"

"There isn't," said Terry, briefly. "They were milestones."

Don swallowed.

"M-m-milestones?" he asked his eyes bulging. Then he subsided into silence.

Ahead of them the green Hillman tore along, over a railway crossing, round a bend in the road, along the next stretch, and then, suddenly the driver slackened speed, turned off the road on to a comparatively narrow dirt road, and, in a few moments, was pulling up outside a small, pleasant-looking red-brick building, with large glass windows, and, in front, a small, neat lawn with flowering scarlet geraniums in big stone pots at the corners.

The building was obviously offices, for at the back, a long concrete building was a factory. From it came the loud hum of machinery, and numbers of African workmen were constantly going in and out through the wide doors.

The driver of the Hillman got out, and strolled into the road to wave the M.G. to a stop.

As Terry braked to a standstill, the small man walked up to them, sunlight glinting on his spectacles.

"I thought I didn't know your car," he said, unexpectedly.

Terry got out of the car.

"I didn't imagine you did," he said, pleasantly. "May I have a word with you?"

"My office isn't private, if that's what you want," said the little man. "So this is as good a place as any other. In any case, I've nothing to hide. But I'd like to know who you are first."

Terry put a hand in his pocket and pulled out a wallet from which he extracted a visiting card and handed it to the man.

The man read it and glanced up.

"The police?" he said sharply. "What's it all about?"

"May I have your name?" said Terry.

"Certainly. Paul Carruthers. I live in Norton— The Gables—with my wife and two small sons. I'm the industrial chemist for this firm. I've been here for the past three or four years."

"You were in Salisbury this morning?"

"Certainly. As a matter of fact, a very interesting point cropped up in connection with a certain experiment. There was a difference of opinion between myself and my colleagues, so I ran into Salisbury to the Queen Victoria Memorial Library. I knew they had a copy of *Atoms of Man*, and I had mislaid mine. I checked the point I wanted, and I came straight back. I saw you following me when I passed the showground— and you were still following me when I turned off the main road. May I ask why?"

"A case of mistaken identity, sir," said Terry, politely.

He and the small man strolled towards the office building, and disappeared through the door.

When they appeared again, the small man was laughing, and Terry and he parted with every evidence of friendliness.

Terry climbed back into the car.

"Quite genuine," he said, briefly, as he started up the car and turned her round towards the main road.

"Not Mr. X after all?" inquired Don. "Dear me! Still, it's been a nice outing, hasn't it?"

"So we're back where we started," said Terry, as he

finished explaining about Mr. Carruthers. "What does that clue say, anyway?"

"Clue?" asked June.

"The one you got out of the book," said Terry.

June looked at Julie and they both turned a delicate shade of pink.

"We—we were just sorting it out," said Julie.

Terry turned to stare at them.

"To save everybody any further trouble," explained Don. "It's a case of mistaken identity, I think. Julie thought June had it, June thought Julie had it, and then they both thought I had it. In fact, it must be still in the book."

It was several moments before Terry could speak. Then he merely made one short statement.

"So we go back to the library," he said.

"We—we're awfully sorry," murmured the twins.

Terry grinned at them.

"It's my fault as much as anybody's," he said. "I ought to have made certain of it before we followed the pseudo Mr. X."

"You weren't to know that it wasn't really Mr. X," said Julie, warmly. "I can't think how we could have been so silly."

"Let's hope it's still in the book," added June.

"Hush, child," put in Don. "There's a time and a place for everything, and this is not—repeat very definitely not—the time for that sort of remark. Good gracious dearie me, it's made me go all goosegogs——I mean, gooseflesh. You know, the pimply kind."

"There's no reason why it shouldn't still be in the

book," said Terry. "Even if it had been dropped on the floor, whoever picked it up would simply hand it to the librarian. This isn't a ker-rime story, you know, with bands of crooks, and gangs of thugs, and swarms of snatch men all waiting round the corner."

"Just as well, probably," said Don. "I don't feel we're at all up to that form."

The twins were laughing, but Julie looked a little wistful.

"It would be rather fun, wouldn't it," she said. "I mean, I don't think I'd mind the odd gangster—you know."

"You horrible child," murmured Terry.

"Oh, nothing fearfully violent—but, since we're in the middle of an adventure, it wouldn't do it any harm to have a gangster in it, would it?"

"There aren't any gangsters of that kind in Salisbury," said Don. "Terry and I spend our lives looking for them. He wants to catch one so that they'll make him a Chief Detective-Inspector right away, and I want to catch one so that I can scoop the Southern African press and see banner headlines in every paper with my name in lights underneath."

"And the Agency, in gratitude, will make him editor of the Little Darmstadt Pioneer which comes out once a week, price tuppence or three mealies," added Terry.

"Meanwhile, let's get back to the library," said June. "I only hope that clue's all right."

"It will be," said Don, and was silent, not from inclination, but because Terry put his foot flat down, and the M.G. shot forward at a speed which surprised even the driver.

In what seemed only a few minutes, he slackened for the streets of Salisbury, and, having managed to scrape through the traffic lights, they were once more within sight of the library.

Terry turned the car in through the gates before he realised that he should have driven straight on and ignored the building completely.

As he pulled up outside the big building, a dozen young men came surging round the car.

Some had cameras, some had notebooks, and all were talking at once.

Hurriedly Don laid a hand on the shoulders of the twins.

"Stay where you are and say nothing," he muttered, and climbed out of the car.

"Hey, chaps, what on earth is this?" demanded Terry, as he and Don with one accord leant casually on the bonnet of the car, almost completely hiding the twins.

There was a chorus of: "Did you get Mr. X?" and much laughter.

"He doesn't live at Norton," called out one horn-rimmed, grey-flannelled gentleman, fingering a camera.

There was another laugh.

"Come on, give us a story," said a tall, thin, older man. "What's the set-up here?"

"Look, just a minute, chaps," cut in Don, shifting his position to foil a photographer in his effort to take a picture of the twins. "Where did you get this Norton idea from?"

"Gent by the name of Carruthers," explained the older man. "He's a pal of Jim's—you know, you mustn't hide this sort of thing from us. Carruthers phoned Jim, didn't he?"

"That's right," said Jim. "He thought it a terrific joke being mistaken for Mr. X. He rang me up and told me you'd chivvied him all the way from the library. It sounded like a good story, so I came to have a look-see, just in case you were casting back here. These vultures sort of ganged up on the thing."

He jerked his head at his fellow reporters.

"Well, I'm sorry, but there's nothing in it at the moment," said Terry, firmly. "In any case, I'm only tidying up the odds and ends on the Mr. X case—Inspector Briggs is the man you want, and you know that."

"He can't tell us anything," said the bespectacled young man. "He's like a bloodhound that's lost the scent. And you don't tidy up odds and ends by chasing somebody to Norton, Terry."

" *With* an Agency man as co-driver, I suppose, in case you got tired," called out another reporter.

"Who are the youngsters?" inquired another photographer.

Don took a deep breath and walked towards the group.

"Look," he said. " Do me a favour and drop that angle. Those two are just friends of mine. They came along for the ride."

There was a chorus of annoyance and disbelief.

"This is getting us nowhere," went on Don, steadily.

"You know perfectly well you can't print a story without the Inspector's consent, or everything in this town will drop on you."

"Just try us," said a voice.

"There's no story at the moment," cut in Terry. "But there may be fairly soon."

"Then you are on to something," said the man called Jim.

"Maybe—maybe not—it's not in any shape to talk about at the moment," said Terry. "As soon as it is——"

"As soon as it is, Don scoops it, doesn't he?" demanded the bespectacled young man.

Terry glanced at Don, and Don nodded.

"Not this time," he said. "I'll do a deal with you fellows. Give me twenty-four hours—leave these youngsters out of it—and I'll see you get a story. Print something now and you'll wreck the whole set-up. Is it a deal?"

The little group muttered together for a moment or two, and then they fanned out again to face the two men.

"It's a deal," said the older man. "Twenty-four hours, Terry. But, if you don't come clean at the end of that time, so help me we'll bust the thing wide open —pictures and all—with those youngsters, too. I've a pretty good idea who they are, and, in any case, twins aren't so difficult to find in this town—we can always check with the schools, in case you think of hiding them."

"Are you threatening?" asked Terry, very quietly.

The older man smiled back at him pleasantly. "No, of course not," he said. "Only explaining."

"Come on, chaps," said Jim. "There's nothing here just now. Twenty-four hours, Terry."

"Twenty-four hours," agreed Terry.

"And give my love to the inspector," added the older man.

"Give my love to Mr. Carruthers," said Don, and watched as the little group sauntered across to the car park and piled into the two or three cars standing there.

In a moment they were gone, and Don was mopping his brow.

"That was a near thing" he said. "May all the plagues fall upon Mr. Carruthers for blowing the gaff."

"It's something I never thought of," said Terry. "Fancy bringing down the entire Press on us like that —with cameramen."

"May we come out now," said June, in a small voice.

"Yes," nodded Terry. "Let's get that clue and get out of here, quick."

"In case they change their minds?" asked Julie.

"They won't do that," said Don. "They'll play fair. They're not a bad crowd, really. Only they get a bit out of hand when they smell a really good story."

"I thought you were supposed to be having the story, if and when it turns up," said Julie, as she climbed out of the car.

"I was—I'm not any longer," growled Don. "Anyway, not as a scoop. I dare say I shall gather a few crumbs from it which the others won't pick up, but it's not the same thing."

"It's our fault," said June. "If we hadn't left the clue here, we wouldn't have had to come back, and this wouldn't have happened."

"Don't worry over that," laughed Don. "I know those lads. If we hadn't turned up here, they'd have tracked us down—probably you'd have found one in your bath this evening. I know them. Give them a smell of a story, and nothing'll pull them off it unless a bigger story comes along. No, don't worry about it."

"He's quite right," agreed Terry. "We'll do better to concentrate on the next twenty-four hours. Come along—let's get this clue."

Obediently they all trooped into the library once more and went straight through the archway into the second room and along to the far end, where they had first found the book.

The volume was still in its place, and the twins quickly pulled it out and shook the leaves.

"It's still there," said Julie, in tones of relief, as a white envelope fluttered to the floor.

"Oh, I am glad," said June. "I was a bit worried in spite of all you said about it's being certain to be here."

Don bent down to pick up the envelope. He glanced at the superscription.

"To the Twins," he read. "That's all right. It's for you."

He handed it to them, and Julie took it and turned it over to pull out the card.

"Just a moment," said Terry, quickly. "Wasn't that sealed?"

The twins looked up at him, a little startled at the tone of his voice.

"Yes, of course—no—I don't know," stammered Julie.

She glanced down at the envelope.

"It's not now," she said, and lifted the flap easily.

"Just let me have a look at that," said Terry. "Take out the card and give me the envelope."

Julie eased out the now familiar white card and handed the envelope to Terry.

She and her sister read the card, eyes wide with surprise, while Don watched Terry as he carefully took the envelope, lifted the flap and examined the underneath.

He looked up and caught Don's eye.

He nodded in answer to the question he saw there.

"Yes," he said. "It's been licked down, and later opened—look, you can see where the flap's been eased up—probably with a knife. Very neatly done."

"But the clue's still in it—I mean, we've only just taken it out," said June.

"Somebody else has had a look at it first," said Terry, quietly.

"What's the clue?" asked Don.

"Oh, awful—but different," said Julie, and handed him the card.

Quickly he read it through and then turned it over.

"Have you read the back?" he asked.

The twins shook their heads and he handed it back to them.

"*Dear Twins*," June read aloud. "*This is the last clue— after all, they must stop some time. It's been great fun, though. If you can solve this final effort, you can add another ten marks to your I.Q. rating. What's more you'll find everything neatly finalised. Auf wiedersehen, though I don't think we shall. And thanks for a lot of fun. Mr. X.*"

She turned the card over again.

"It's a sort of arithmetic problem—not a rhyming clue this time," added Julie, as she looked at it.

Terry took Don by the arm.

"Listen," he said. "I've a feeling we've got to work fast. Take these two over to the Park, Don, and get them working on it. You can have some coffee or something and sit down at a table there. For goodness sake, don't leave them, even for a moment. And stay there until you get a message from me or I turn up myself. I'm going to try and find out who opened that envelope."

"You think somebody really did?" asked Julie.

"I'm sure of it," said Terry. "Opened it—and read that clue. Now off you go—and for goodness sake, solve that clue quickly."

"Right you are," said Don. "We'll stay there till you turn up, or we hear from you. Don't worry. They'll be safe with me. You know me—the human guard—guaranteed to repel all oncomers. Be seeing you."

Terry grinned and lifted a hand in acknowledgment as Don put his arms through those of the girls and fairly lifted them down the room, under the archway, out of the library and across the road to the Park, where, in the distance, surrounded with banks of gay flowers and tall trees, the long, low shape of the tea house could be seen with the bright tables and umbrellas grouped round it.

CHAPTER VIII

A SUCCESSFUL SOLUTION

IN A VERY short time, the three were sitting round a small table, set rather far apart from the others. It was covered by a bright check tablecloth, and suitable refreshments were set out on it.

The sun was bright and unusually warm for the time of year, but the big umbrella shaded them from its direct rays.

The luncheon crowd had gone back to their various offices, and the Park was almost deserted.

On a distant stretch of closely-cropped green grass, two small children romped, while an African nanny, in a blue overall and turban watched them as she sat on the grass.

Screened behind enormous flowering purple bougain-villaeas, the children in the small amusement park could be heard shouting gleefully as they played on the swings or rode on the wheel.

Odd cries came from the collection of cages in the far corner of the Park, where some peacocks, a tame duiker and various other animals were housed and overfed by the adoring public.

" D'you know that we've missed lunch altogether," said Don, as the African waiter came up to their table.

"Well, we did nothing but eat all the morning at Mermaid's, so I don't think we're really hungry," laughed June.

"Oh, nonsense," snorted Don. "You've got to keep your strength up if you're going to struggle successfully with that little bunch of brain-fag."

And, paying no attention to the protestations of the twins, he ordered an enormous meal of cold meat, avocado pear salad, rolls and butter, coffee, and finished off with guavas and cream.

"We shall simply go fast asleep if we eat that lot," declared Julie, severely.

"You've got that bit wrong," Don pointed out, seriously. "I shall go to sleep—you will both be working hard. There's a never-ending supply of ice to be had here when you wish to apply it to your fevered brows. As my great-uncle always said—the cooling of the brain deceives the fever—or something like it."

"I don't think that's quite right," laughed June.

"Probably not. It was in his day that they finally gave up breaking the ice in the local pond before he went in for a swim. Before that, he kept a couple of footmen for the purpose. Footmen are excellent for breaking the ice, you know. Far better than a sledge hammer which, after all, only splinters the surface. However, the R.S.P.C.A. objected, and he eventually gave it up and used a kettle of hot water carefully poured over a small portion of the ice. It wasn't as satisfactory, but, after all, he never needed a big hole through which to plunge. He was a very small man and he never dipped more than his big toe into the water."

"Good gracious, after all that trouble? Why ever not?" asked Julie.

"Great-aunt's orders," said Don, seriously. "She was better than any doctor. It was she who insisted that he should never take exercise on an empty stomach, and you know, he never did and he lived to be ninety-five all out. For that matter, he used to take medicine, not exercise, but, on the one or two occasions when exercise was all he could find to take, he used a spoon, never an empty stomach. And here's our lea," he added, as the waiter approached with a laden tray.

"Lea?" chorused the twins.

"That's right. Lunch and tea combined. Same as breakfast and lunch, eaten with a pinch of salt in mid-morning, is always called brunch."

"Oughtn't we to be getting on with that clue?" asked Julie, as she picked up her knife and fork.

"All in good time," said Don, firmly. "Remember the old proverb, haste not, want not. You've got to be fed."

"But Terry——" began June.

"Terry is perfectly happy chasing imaginary gangsters," laughed Don.

"Imaginary?" asked the girls.

"I think so," said Don. "I'm quite certain there's no criminals on our tail—why should there be? What would they be after? You're not hunting for the long-lost treasure of the Whiffenpooffels, or the missing crown jewels of Ruritania. Terry's only worry is to have everything tied up neatly before this time to-morrow, when that bunch of jackals falls upon him again."

"You mean, he wants the case finished, Mr. X in his hands and so on before to-morrow?" asked June.

Don nodded.

"That's it. Inspector Briggs is the big boss, but don't let young Terry fool you. He's really handling the case, and he's all set not only to lay hands on the thief, but to get back the goods—swag—proceeds of said robbery—etc."

"And, if he can't give the Press a story by to-morrow?" asked Julie.

"Then everything breaks loose," said Don. "You can't hold those boys back for too long. We've all got to explain to our editors if we fall down on a story— and they've no intention of falling down on it. It'll mean front-page headlines, pictures of you two, where you live, how you live, full details of all the clues— even Rhodesian Newsreel will probably crash in on it."

The girls shuddered.

"We'd never live it down," said Julie.

"And goodness only knows what the parents would say," added June.

"Exactly," said Don. "That's why he stalled just now."

There was a moment's silence, while the twins thoughtfully ate their salad.

"That's what you were going to do, isn't it, Don?" asked Julie, at last.

"What? Pictures of you two and the rest? Good

heavens, no," said Don, in horrified tones. "I was only chasing the story from the Mr. X angle. I wouldn't have brought you two into it."

"But you wanted to get the story before anybody else, didn't you?" asked June.

"And you couldn't, because letting the others have the story to-morrow was the only way to stop them taking photographs of us then and there," added Julie.

A curious shade of dull red flooded Don's face, and he shifted uncomfortably in his chair.

"Oh, nonsense," he said. "You've got the wrong end of the stick. That's the luck of the game, as my sister used to say. She played half-back in her school cricket team, you know. They called her the tank for obvious reasons."

"Don't be ridiculous," giggled June. "You don't play half-back at cricket."

Don's eyes opened wide.

"Don't you?" he said, in apparent astonishment. "Perhaps that's why they never won—she could never score any goals for her side. It was sheer persecution on the part of the opposing team, of course. They used to hide the goal-posts, and you can't score a goal if you can't find the goal-posts."

"Just the same," said Julie, when they had finished laughing. "Just the same, we do know—and we're both awfully grateful, Don."

"Yes, well—never mind that. Have some more to eat," said Don.

"Oh, we couldn't eat another thing," declared June.

"Well, have a cigarette—no, you don't smoke at your tender age, of course. Have a peppermint—have some stomach tablets? They're a great aid to indigestion, I find."

"Don, tell us why you don't think there's a crook involved," said Julie. "Who d'you think opened the envelope if it wasn't someone who wanted to know what the clue was?"

"I think it was sheer curiosity on the part of somebody who saw what happened," said Don.

"But there wasn't anybody *to* see," exclaimed Julie.

"Oh, yes, there was," contradicted Don. "There were three people in the library itself, apart from the staff. There were two youngsters in that second room we were in. There may have been others, too."

"We never saw anybody at all," declared June.

"Ah, well that's where my Scout training comes in, you know," explained Don. "We were always trained to those sort of things."

"What sort of things?" asked June.

"Like rubbing two cubs together to find water, and playing last man off with the mosquitoes at camp. It's most exciting. The mosquitoes have to bite you once before they take off, and, if you can slap them down before they get that bite, then it's one point and a dead mosquito to you. Then there was Kim's game."

"Oh, yes, we've heard of that," said June, solemnly.

"That's right," nodded Don. "You're shown a huge shop window full of about five thousand and twenty-four objects. Then you're led away and told to write down not less than five thousand and forty four of the objects you remember seeing in the shop window if you can write while you're forgetting to remember. I've often thought I'd like to meet Kim. I'd teach him a game. And now," he went on. "If you're finished the preliminary stages of digestion, let's start, will you?"

At a signal, the waiter cleared the table, leaving only a pot of coffee for Don, and two tall glasses of iced orange for the girls.

Don pulled a notebook out of his pocket and a couple of pencils, just as the twins were feeling in the big pockets of their skirts.

"Oh, aren't you clever!" exclaimed June. "Just what we want."

"Can I have that in triplicate?" asked Don. "And take care of that notebook. We don't want a paper-chase through the Park this afternoon, so treasure every sheet."

"And now let's really study the clue," said Julie, producing the card.

It was not, as they had noticed, a rhyming clue as the others had been. Instead, there were two questions on it, carefully numbered.

A read: *What is $1\frac{1}{2} \div \frac{3}{4}$?*

B read: *What is the largest amount of loose silver you can have without being able to give exact change for £1?*

Don read them with starting eyes. Then he laid down the card on the table and sat back.

"Will you have the ice now or in five minutes?" he inquired.

"We'll have a go first," giggled June. "Aren't you going to help us?"

"Me?" squealed Don. "Don't be absurd. Why, I can't even add up. I always include the date or the number I first thought of. As for subtraction, the only problem in subtraction I've ever been able to do is the one beginning ' Take a dog from a bone '—and the answer's a nasty bite on one leg. But I'm really hot on division. I can divide a loaf by a knife and get bread and dripping if the dripping's not too hard to spread. No, my little dears. That is entirely your problem. I'm very good at history, but I stop short of that sort of mental cruelty."

He sat back in his chair and lit a cigarette, while the twins each took some sheets of paper and a pencil, and settled down to work.

" Anyway," added Don, after a few moments. " Anyway, what sort of clue is it? It's not going to give you a place to go to, is it?"

"Hush!" said the twins loudly, and, rather chastened, he sat back once more.

For a time, the twins worked silently. By common consent, June was tackling the first problem, and Julie the second.

Their pencils scribbled figures endlessly over the paper, and every so often one or other of them would mutter furiously, crumple up the sheet she had been writing on, and, taking a fresh page, start again.

"Better try it with x," declared Julie, pushing her curls back.

"Why?" asked Don.

"No, x," she said, crossly.

" Oh, I see," he murmured.

She looked at him and sighed with exasperation.

"Listen," she said, slowly. "When you're doing algebra, you always start with x as the unknown quantity. Not o, or i, or c, or y, or any other of the twenty something letters of the alphabet. X—always X, see?"

"No," said Don, loudly. "You've got your facts wrong. And, anyway, you can't say you always use x, and then tell me you use x c. It's just not done."

"1 didn't say x c," retorted Julie. "I said you always use x, see?"

"Why bring a u into it?" demanded Don, furiously.

"Who's bringing a u into it?" asked Julie.

"You are," he answered.

"You said a u—now you say u r. What do you think you're doing?" she said.

Don heaved an enormous sigh.

"Shall we try it in Russian, or would you rather set it to music, and play it? I'm a devil on the tenor sax," he said.

Julie laughed helplessly.

"We'll settle for x," she said, firmly. "And now, do me a favour and stop, please? I'm nearly there, I think. But I can't concentrate when you behave like that."

Don assumed an injured air.

"In that case, I shall be silent as the grave," he announced. "No word shall sully my lips—no——"

"Be QUIET" shrieked June. "How on earth can I concentrate——"

"Yes, that's where I came in," said Don. "You can skip the rest. I've heard it already from your sister.

And now, are you going to get that solved to-day, or do we tell the Press now?"

With an awful look, the twins again bent their heads and went to work once more.

Presently, June looked up.

"I think the answer's two," she said.

Julie glanced up at her.

"Have you got it?" she asked. "Jolly good."

"WHAT?" screeched Don. "Here—let me have a look at the question."

He reached across the table for the card, and read it.

"Oh, you're wrong," he said, curtly. "You're way off the beam. You've got brain fever—I knew it would happen. Waiter—ice—quickly?"

"Don, be quiet," laughed June.

"No, no, it's serious—ice is the only thing. Restoratives, you know. Ice—strong, sweet tea—shock treatment. It's for me. I've had the shock. Come on, there, hurry up."

In a moment, three waiters were rushing across. One of them carried a tray of glasses, the second was bringing a large jug of water, while the third had a bowl of ice.

The twins were laughing helplessly, but Don continued to issue a stream of orders, and the waiters, grinning from ear to ear, their teeth gleaming white in their black faces, were trotting to and fro with cool fruit drinks, a tray of tea for one, a small saucer on which reposed two aspirin, a packet of cigarettes, some chocolates and finally four straws.

To their intense delight, Don swallowed the aspirin, poured out a cup of tea into which he tipped half the sugar basin, solemnly handed the girls the ice, and put the straws in his hair.

When order had been restored, he started again.

"Let's take this thing calmly," he said.

"We're both quite calm," said Julie, though her voice shook slightly with repressed mirth.

"Very well, then. Now, the first question. Divide $1\frac{1}{2}$ by $\frac{3}{4}$. Am I right?"

"Yes," agreed the twins.

"Then the answer can't possibly be two."

"It can and it is," said June, stubbornly. "You try it and see what you make it?"

"Don't be unpleasant," said Don. "There's no need to be like that. I know the answer, anyway."

"What is it?" asked the girls.

"Four eighths," said Don, firmly.

"There's no such thing," said Julie, laughing. "Four eighths is two fourths which is one half. But you've got to divide one and one half, and the answer couldn't possibly be just one half."

"Stop confusing me," said Don. "I'm getting all mixed up with one and one and one and half and half. And the answer is not a half. Of course it isn't. I know that as well as you. And I didn't say that. I said four eighths."

"But that *is* a half," shrieked June.

"And, anyway, the answer's two," added Julie.

Don cleared his throat.

"Look," he said. "This piece of ice is one. Agreed?"

Staring at the table, where Don was clearing a space, the girls nodded agreement.

"Right. Now this spoon is a half," went on Don. "Agreed?"

Again the girls nodded.

"Good. Now you have to divide that by three-quarters—this teapot is the three-quarters. All right? Still with me?"

"Ye-es," said the twins.

"Very well. You divide the ice and the spoon by the tea-pot—and what's the answer?"

"A milk shake," suggested Julie, and the girls collapsed in helpless laughter.

"Of course, you're not trying," said Don, severely. "Or, if you prefer it the other way, you're very trying."

He swept the three objects away, and picked up the straws.

"We'll try again," he said. "Now pay attention."

Solemnly he broke one straw in half and laid it by the side of a full-length straw. Then he took a third straw and broke off a small piece, which he threw away.

"Now, then," he began. "This 'ere straw is one. And this 'ere straw is a n'arf. O.K.?"

"O.K.," said the girls.

"Right. Now this 'ere three-quarter as near as makes no difference is to be divided by this 'ere one and a n'arf," he went on.

"No, it isn't," said June. "It's the other way round. You divide the one and a half by the three-quarters."

"That's what I said," declared Don.

"Nonsense—you twisted it round. Look—one and a half—divided by three-quarters," said June, as she laid the three-quarter length of straw across the other two.

"And the answer's two," added Julie.

"The answer's a straw mat," snapped Don, and swept the straws into a heap.

"It's no good—the answer's two," declared June.

"Look—if I divide my bank balance by three-quarters, d'you think I get two bank balances?" demanded Don. "Because, if that's the case, you'd better come and see my bank manager to-morrow."

"Supposing you divide your overdraft by three-quarters—you might get two overdrafts," said Julie, softly. " I should be careful."

"Remove that child," said Don, excitedly. "Take her away and teach her proper respect for her elders. Why, if my second cousin twice removed—though we never could discover who removed her—if my cousin as before could hear you, she'd——"

"Never mind about your cousin hearing you—I can hear you half across the Park," said a voice.

The three looked up to see Terry grinning down at them.

"Why, we never heard you," said Julie.

" Didn't you know? He's really Fairy Lightfoot," said Don. "Anyway I'm glad to see you. You've arrived in the nick of time—the crucial moment—the——"

" All right. I've arrived," said Terry, sitting down. "Let's skip the rest."

"But how rude!" said Don, reproachfully. "Never mind. These two ornaments of the nature class have solved the first problem. They've divided one and a half by three-quarters and made the answer two. And they've also gone purblind. They refuse to see the error of their ways. Here have I been—trying to educate them—trying gently but firmly to explain——"

"Oh, nonsense," said Julie. "You'd got to the stage of throwing things at us."

"You drove me to it," said Don. "I keep telling you that——"

"They're quite right," said Terry, quietly.

"I keep telling——" repeated Don and then stopped to turn and stare at Terry.

"What did you say?" he demanded.

"They're quite right. The answer's two."

Don looked round, a frightened expression on his face.

"It must be catching," he said. "Something in the air—perhaps. I—I—excuse me, I'm afraid I've got to go now. An urgent appointment. I——"

He half-rose from his chair, and Terry, laughing, pulled him down again.

"Don't be absurd," he said. "If you can't work it out at this moment, save it for a nice quiet evening at home. Meanwhile, let's save a little time, will you, and accept it that the answer's two."

Don stared at him.

"Are you sure you feel all right, old boy?" he asked, tenderly. "No headaches, spots before the eyes, night starvation? Is your internal rhythm——"

"That'll do," said Terry. "The answer's two. Let's leave it at that. What about the second problem?"

"As far as I can see," said Julie, picking up the last sheet of paper she had been using. "As far as I can see, the largest amount of change you can get in silver without being able to give exact change is seven half-crowns, four two-shilling-pieces and a tickey, which totals twenty-five shillings and ninepence. If you add any other silver coin to it, then you can give the exact change."

"I don't mind," said Don. "The tickey will just do nicely for the parking meter."

Terry picked up the sheet of paper and studied her calculations.

"That looks right to me," he said. "You can't add another half-crown, and you certainly can't add any more florins. If you bring in a bob, it splits the thing wide open."

"It's a way bobs have," said Don. "I remember I was bobbing for apples one day, and the wretched thing swung back and split my front teeth wide open. One pointed north and the other west, and Mother was furious!"

"Yes, I think that's the answer," said Terry, ignoring him. "Twenty-five shillings and ninepence."

The twins looked at him.

"But—where does that get us?" asked June. "Twenty five shillings and ninepence and a two."

Terry frowned for a moment. Then he shook his head and laughed.

"It's the other way round," he said. "The two comes first."

"What difference does that make?" asked June. "Or do you multiply the 25/9d. with the two? Which gives us 51/6d."

"Just the price of a packet of cigarettes," said Don. "Which reminds me."

He leant across and helped himself to a cigarette from the box in Terry's pocket.

"But that's no answer—no clue," said Julie.

"I think it is," nodded Terry. "It's the last clue. This gives you the final answer."

"I know," said Don, brilliantly. "It's the rising cost of living, and the answer is to be found in the Stats Office."

"The Stats Office?" chorused the girls.

"Statistics, my little dears," said Don. "They're the fellows who'll show you how to divide two and five-eights by seven and four-fifths and make it two hundred and forty-four."

Terry picked up a pencil and wrote the four figures down on the sheet of paper. Then he handed it to them.

The three bent to stare at it.

"Two—two—five—nine," read Julie and looked at Terry.

"It's a phone number," said June. "Is that it?"

"Not quite," said Terry. "The city phones are all five numbers and none of the outside exchanges begin with a two. No—try again."

"Street numbers—flat numbers—plot numbers. Plot numbers?" asked June, looking up.

"Could be, but I don't think it's likely. It'd be too difficult to trace, and I don't think, at this stage, Mr. X is trying to make it too difficult. Try once more."

Don glanced at Terry, an eyebrow raised, and Terry grinned back. Then they looked at the twins.

"I know," said June suddenly. "A box number— a post office box number. Is that it?"

"I think so," said Terry.

"Good girl," nodded Don. "Come along and let's get down to the Post Office right away."

"But—but the post office boxes are all locked and we haven't got the key," protested Julie.

"Never mind. You stick by your Uncle Don and then you can see how the great detective opens a box without a key. It's magic, really—not the usual abracadabra, of course. It's a secret word he murmurs into the lock, and the lock is so shocked about him knowing it that it flies right open and there you are."

"Oh, nonsense," laughed June. "Can you really open the box?"

"Yes," said Terry. "But not like that."

They were walking towards the gates of the Park, outside which the red car could be seen parked in the shade of a flame tree.

"The boxes aren't locked at the back," explained Terry. "The door is locked, of course, but when you open it in the normal way, you can see that there is only a short piece at the back, and the rest is a wide slit."

"A slit?" asked June.

"Yes. The other side of the boxes is the wall of the sorting room," went on Terry. "The Post Office sorters simply push the letters and things through the slit and they drop into the box."

"Oh, I see," said Julie. "So the box is only locked at the front, so that the public can't open it, but the sorters at the back can get to it quite easily."

"That's right," said Terry. "You've got it in one."

"And the fact that Terry is no sorter makes not the slightest difference," added Don. "He merely goes into the Sorters' room which is strictly and heavily marked 'No Admittance' and dazzles them with his policeman's personality. The rest, of course, is easy."

Before anybody could reply, he was urging them into the car, and in a few moments, they were driving down to the centre of the city where the huge bulk of the General Post Office could be seen from the other end of the tree-lined street.

Once again Terry parked the car, and the four got out and walked round the outside of the building until they reached the long narrow hall where the lines of Post Office boxes were built into the walls.

It was nearly five o'clock, and there was an air of intense activity over the whole place.

Native messengers with canvas bags full of letters were busily pushing them through the slots of the big posting boxes, according to their destinations or whether they bore the blue air-mail stickers.

Other Africans were opening various Post Boxes and emptying them of their contents before shutting and re-locking them. Europeans were moving in and out all the time, their hands full of letters and parcels, and the air was filled with the noise and chatter of the crowd, the deep, guttural accents of the Africans mingling with the lighter tones of the Europeans, while, over all, was the noise of the constant opening and shutting of the little metal doors.

Their eyes on the numbered boxes, the little group made their way up the hall, past the big swing doors that led into the main part of the Post Office, and on until they finally reached the box marked with the engraved figures 2259.

It was in the third row, with two rows above and two rows below it, and it looked harmless enough as they stared at it.

"What now?" asked Julie.

Terry glanced at Don.

"Will you stay here with the twins?" he asked. "Just to see nobody tampers with it. I'll go round to the back and get them to let me have a look inside."

Don nodded.

"By this pillar, I think," he said, guiding the two girls to where, a little distance away, a big pillar formed part of the entrance colonnade. "If I may have your newspaper, old boy, we can study the racing news while unobtrusively keeping an eye on our little friend No. 2259."

Terry grinned and handed over the newspaper he was carrying.

"Why—d'you think somebody might go to the Box?" asked Julie. "D'you think Mr. X——?"

"Ssh!" said Don, reprovingly. "The Great Man is taking no chances, that's all. He remembers what he learnt at Mr. Sherlock Holmes's knee, that's all. Off you go, Terry, and don't be too long. These two will shortly blow up if they don't find out what's in that Box."

Terry laughed and nodded.

"I won't be long," he said, and moved away quickly, becoming lost in the crowd.

"Now come and look at the paper," said Don firmly. "I'll give you the strip cartoon if you're good. And don't watch that box too openly."

Obediently the girls took the sheet that he handed them and looked at the cartoon, while Don glanced at the rest of the paper. He had seen it before, and the twins had read the cartoon through carefully three times without having grasped a word of what it meant, when there was a sudden surge of people.

Two or three pushed past, brushing the girls as they went. In a moment they had dispersed, and there was just the normal scurrying to and fro.

But Julie had jumped back with a cry.

"My pocket," she said. "Somebody took——"

She slipped a hand into the wide pocket of her skirt and her fingers encountered a small, cold object.

Slowly she pulled her hand out and stared at the little key she was holding.

"Nobody took—somebody put," said Don, and took the key from her.

On the handle the figures 2259 were engraved.

"It's—it's the key to the postbox," gasped June.

"Who dropped it in—did you see?" asked Don, quickly.

But Julie shook her head.

"I've not the remotest idea," she said. "I just felt something on my skirt—I thought somebody had tried to take something out of my pocket. But I've no idea who."

"There were three or four people all rushing past," added June. "It was just a group of people, sort of thing. You couldn't spot anybody, and we weren't actually looking, either."

Don was craning his neck to see over the heads of the people.

"Whoever it was, they've gone now," he said, disappointed. "Anyway—you might as well open the box."

Eagerly, the twins ran across to the box, and Julie inserted the key and twisted it in the lock.

The door swung back and, as she reached a hand in to pick up the rather bulky parcel that was the only thing in the box, Terry's hand came through from the other side.

"I've got it, Terry," she cried.

Terry stared at her, in surprise. But he wasted no words.

"Just stay where you are," he said, curtly. "Lock that box again, and stay with Don. I'll be right round."

Quickly, the girls locked the box and moved back to the pillar with Don. In a surprisingly short time, Terry was back with them.

He glanced once at the parcel in Julie's hand.

"My office is round the corner in the next building," said Don, softly. "Let's get out of this, shall we?"

Terry nodded, and the little group moved away.

Three minutes later, they were all sitting in Don's office, high above the roar of traffic from the street, with only the mutter of voices, the occasional shrill of a telephone bell and the constant chatter of the telegraph machines breaking the silence.

The two men watched the girls as they opened the parcel. It was carefully sealed with scotch tape, and, even when the brown paper covering was removed, there were two more layers of thinner paper.

But at last they had unwrapped it, and inside were two small boxes, and a large envelope addressed to the twins.

Leaving the boxes for the moment, they opened the letter and pulled out a sheet of notepaper and a second envelope.

"Shall I read it?" asked Julie, and Terry nodded.

"'*My dear Twins*,'" she read, obediently. "'*This is good-bye, of course. Thanks for giving me a lot of fun——I certainly enjoyed the clues and I hope you did, too. Do me a last favour and give the enclosed to your friend, the policeman. He'll know what to do with it. The enclosed for memory's sake. Mr. X.*'"

She stared at Terry in bewilderment, while June picked up the second envelope and handed it to him.

Quickly he ripped it open and pulled out a large, closely-written sheet of paper.

He glanced through it quickly. Then he picked up the telephone, dialled a number in silence, and, when he got an answer, gave some instructions briefly to the person at the other end, finishing up with a request to get in touch with him at the Agency office as soon as possible.

He hung up the receiver, glanced at Don and the girls, and then back at the letter.

"Just listen to this," he said, quietly, and began to read it aloud.

"'*My dear Detective,*'" he read. "'*It is with great regret that I have to disappoint you. I am not the burglar you are after, and I'm afraid you will never catch him. However, I will lay the facts before you, and you shall judge the curious story for yourself—the truth I can vouch for.*

"'*On the night of the Wilson robbery, I was driving back from a party at the home of a farmer friend of mine. It was quite early, but there was very little traffic on the roads, as it happened.*

"'*Not far from the Wilson house—though I didn't know that at the time, not having had the pleasure of Sir John's acquaintance—I saw a car at the side of the road. The driver was evidently having trouble, for he was bending over, with his head well under the raised bonnet, frantically twiddling with the complicated mechanism you always find in that part of a car.*

"'*I pulled up behind him, got out and walked up to see if I could help him. He never heard me until I asked him what the matter was, and then he jumped like a rabbit. He must have had the deuce of a shock, for he was shaking all over as he turned to face me. Then I had a shock, for I recognised him at once. He was my old batman who'd been through the war with me. Spud, he was called—but not because his surname was Murphy. A quite different reason, which wouldn't interest you, anyway. Towards the end of that little kick-up—1944 it was—we'd had an argument with a shell. I was wounded and when I woke up in hospital, he'd disappeared. Presumed dead. I'd done everything, of course, but I'd never been able to trace him.*

"' And here he was, fiddling with a car that wouldn't go —he was always a fool with engines—by the side of a Rhodesian road one night—and obviously terrified out of his wits.

"' Well, I calmed him down, put the engine to rights—it was a trifling fault—and told him to follow me. I knew he would, he was so darned relieved to see me.

"' I led him back to my small shack, and gave him a stiff drink. Then I heard his story. We'll skip most of it. The bit that would interest you is that he got in with a bad crowd and had finally had to skip the country. Never mind which country. He'd finally landed in Rhodesia, but things weren't too hot. In the end, one way and the other, he'd burgled the Wilson house—he'd done the job properly, got away with quite a packet, and then his car had died on him, and that's where I had strolled in.

"' Well, I couldn't leave him just lying around. I'd got to give him a hand, apart from my delight at finding him again.

" ' I fixed it all up that evening. I was thinking of leaving Rhodesia myself—I've been a bit of a rolling stone since the war—and it seemed a good idea to take him with me. He was only too anxious to do whatever I told him to do—he'd always been like that. It took a few days to fix everything up,

and I kept him hidden at my place, where I knew he wouldn't be found, if luck was with us. But I had to stall the police—hence the first clue. I take it you restored the property to the hotel resident. I handled that myself—my particular wartime training came in useful there.

"' *Then the twins took a hand, I had to go on—of course, I enjoyed it, though I hoped you weren't going to be too brilliant with them.*

"'*Well, now it's over. By the time you read this, Spud and I will have left the country—an early morning plane. Don't worry about him—he'll not do that sort of thing again. You'll find the whole of Sir John's property at No. 8 Jacaranda Road, Highlands.*

" ' *And so, for the last time, my dear Detective, I sign myself—Mr. X*'"

There was a long silence as Terry finished reading the letter.

Then Don swore under his breath.

"What are you worrying about?" asked Terry. "It's still a good story."

"It's not at all good," said Don. "We've got to keep the twins out of it, and you can work out for yourself what the Press are going to say about it. Oh, well, how hard can a reporter's life be. Are you checking on it?"

Terry glanced at his watch.

"Another five minutes, and we'll know," he said. "There's a car going out to Jacaranda Road now. Not that I've much hope."

The twins looked at him.

"You mean, you don't think the stuff will be there?" demanded Julie.

Terry turned to them and shrugged his shoulders. "It's anybody's guess," he said. "This could be just a hoax."

"Of course it isn't," flared June. "Mr. X wouldn't do such a thing. Why, you must know it's all true, every bit of it. And of course you'll get back every last salt spoon. You'll find it all waiting for you—you see."

"All right, all right," said Terry. "I never said we shouldn't. This Mr. X may be one of those quixotic people who behaves like that. I've never met them outside a book before, but you never know."

Don cut in hurriedly as he saw the look of battle in the eyes of the twins.

"Er—what about opening your—er—presents," he suggested.

"Oh, yes, let's," said Julie, and, in a moment, their eager fingers were untying the thin, gold string and prising the lids off the boxes.

Inside each was a good deal of cotton wool, but at last they had pulled it away, and each gave a gasp at what lay on the white velvet base of the boxes.

"It's—oh, it's lovely," gasped Julie, as she lifted out a long, slender gold chain from which hung a small pendant in the shape of a flower, beautifully designed, with delicate petals, the centre of the blossom a single pearl, the whole surrounded by leaves of vivid green enamel.

June's pendant was identical, and the two girls stared in speechless delight at the charming gifts.

"And very nice, too," said Don, eyeing the pendants. "Mr. X certainly has the most attractive ideas."

"Why? Is it a special sort of flower?" asked Julie. Don rolled his eyes upwards and sighed.

"Alas!" he mourned. "Where's your natural history got to? What about those days in junior school when you covered sheets of enormous and expensive drawing paper with petals, calyxes, sepals and so on? And still you don't know that the flower's the rosemary."

"Rosemary?" echoed the girls and looked at Terry.

"I should say he's probably right," nodded Terry.

"Of course I am," retorted Don.

"Rosemary for remembrance," quoted Julie.

"Ah, well, at least you know your Shakespeare," said Don, approvingly. "Othello at his best, I always think."

For once, neither twin took him up on his remark, for they were staring at the small pendants.

"It's—it's lovely," said June, softly.

"Rosemary for remembrance—I think it's charming," agreed Julie.

"We will now sing that ancient and popular hymn," announced Don. "You'll find it in the back of the book. Hymn four hundred and fifty-four. 'Now the gorge is rising'. All together, if you please, and try and keep in time with your sniffles."

"Oh, you are horrible," said Julie, laughing, as she fastened the pendant round her neck.

June had just finished doing the same when there came a knock at the door, and two uniformed policemen came in, immaculate in their khaki tunics and shorts, their brown leather leggings and boots polished to a high degree of brilliance.

They carefully removed their flat, khaki caps and tucked them under their arms.

"We've got it here, sir, if you'd like to check it now," said one of them, and the girls noticed that they had two large and bulky cases with them.

"All right," said Terry. "Everything okay otherwise?"

"Nobody there," said the constable, laying the case on the desk. "It's just a rondavel, all on its own, on a spare bit of land. It's quite deserted. Locked, of course, with the key tucked above the door. Easy to find, though I don't suppose anybody'd bother to break in to a place like that."

"And inside?" asked Terry, as he watched them opening the cases.

"Just a couple of beds, table, couple of chairs, bits and pieces—comfortable, you know, but nothing gilt-edged," said the constable.

"They kept the gilding for this lot," murmured Don and the eyes of the two constables bulged as they lifted the tops off the cases and started to unpack the contents.

"And to think this little lot was just left lying by the side of the table," said the second constable, when he could speak again.

"Safest way," said Terry. "As you say, nobody'd bother to break into a place like that."

Within five minutes the top of the large desk was completely transformed.

The jewellery had been taken out of the jewel boxes by the burglar, Spud, in the first place, and was now carefully wrapped in cotton wool.

Emeralds, rubies, pearls and diamonds winked up at the little group from the white cotton-wool nests in which they lay. Brooches, bracelets, rings, necklaces—there a dazzling ruby and diamond tiara had matching ear-rings, brooches and bracelet, while in another corner a three-string collar of creamy pearls glowed faintly in the light.

At one side, five gold cigarette cases formed a chequer pattern, and in the centre of the desk were grouped small silver cups and gold ornaments, some of obvious age and value.

A tiny and perfect Cinderella coach in gold and enamel was drawn by two miniature ponies, with gleaming ruby eyes, their golden harness studded with sapphires, while the coachman on the box and the footmen at the back wore scarlet enamel liveries buttoned with tiny diamonds.

When he could speak again, Don looked at Terry.

"Would you like to check it now?" he asked. "I've got a list of the missing stuff on me."

"I don't think we'll bother," said Terry, quietly. "The insurance people will have to do it with us, anyway. I'd rather get this stuff under lock and key. It gives me the willies just lying around like this."

The two constables promptly started re-packing the priceless things and stowing them carefully back in the cases.

"I'm with you," agreed Don. "Fancy keeping this little lot at a place like Sir John's. Why, it's no different to any other Rhodesian house, only bigger. I mean, anybody can stroll in and out of it any time they feel like it."

"The stuff was in a safe," Terry pointed out.

Don snorted.

"Which anybody could open, I suppose," he said. "We've never been told the safe was burglar-proof. It was just a large and not particularly adequate wall safe."

"Sir John's going to alter that now," said Terry, with a smile. "He's having a proper one put in which will defy even people like Spud."

"I should think so, too," grumbled Don. "And what are you going to do about Spud—and Mr. X?"

The twins looked up quickly from their examination of a delightful emerald-green frog with topaz eyes who was cheerfully squatting on a large leaf attached to a half-open lily made entirely of pearls.

Terry shrugged his shoulders.

"It's up to the Boss," he said. "Personally, I don't think there's anything we can do, except to check and see if we can trace that these two men did actually leave Rhodesia by plane as they say they are going to in this letter."

"Since you don't know their real names, and you've no proper description of them, it won't get you far," grinned Don.

The twins heaved a small sigh of relief, and handed the frog to one of the constables.

"I think you're right," said Terry, a bit resignedly, He looked at the girls.

"So this is the end of the story," he said, quietly.

"It's been a very exciting story," said Julie, watching the last of the priceless possessions of Sir John Wilson being packed into the case.

Terry nodded to the constables, and instructed them to take the cases down to the police station at once, and notify Inspector Briggs that, as far as he could tell, the cases contained the complete results of the Wilson burglary, and that he himself would be along shortly.

"It's a little frustrating for the police," said Don. "For me, too."

"For you?" queried the girls.

"I'd like to have met Mr. X," he explained. "I think we should have got on well together. I like his sense of humour."

"The sense of humour may be all right," said Terry. "But it's no good to us."

"What a shame!" laughed Julie. "But you can't expect us to be sorry. Actually, we're only too pleased that he got away."

"Of course you are," nodded Terry, with a smile. "And you're only too pleased your Mr. X has turned out not to be a thief, after all."

"Well, we are," agreed June, a little defiantly.

"You can't blame us," added Julie.

"Of course not," said Terry. "And you're perfectly right. It may be very unsatisfactory from a police point of view, but I must say that I, personally, have thoroughly enjoyed this last couple of days. I've had a lot of fun, thanks to you two."

Don cleared his throat and gave a little cough.

"Speaking on behalf of the Puddleton Boilermakers' Association," he began. "I should like to say that those is my sentiments, likewise and notwithstanding."

"Then take a chair," suggested Terry.

"Certainly, old boy," said Don, briskly. "Where would you like me to take it to?"

"Well, we've certainly enjoyed it," said Julie. "And we won't forget your help, either. We'd never have solved those clues without you."

"You'd never have gone to Norton and back, either," said Don.

The twins laughed.

"That poor Mr. Carruthers," said Julie. "I'll never forget his face."

"Poor, nothing," snorted Terry. "I won't forget it either, miserable creature. Phoning his pal and letting the story out like that, and bringing that bunch of reporters down on us like—like——"

"The Assyrian is the word you want," said Don. "You know, he got into his party clothes and turned into Red Riding Hood's big bad wolf."

"We shan't forget the shock we got when you suddenly handed us that envelope at Ewanrigg," laughed June.

"Or when Don suddenly turned up at Mermaid's," added Julie.

"That shook me, too," admitted Terry.

"Never mind," said Don. "The solace of my presence,

and the pure sunshine of my personality soon over-whelmed you."

"Well, there we are," said Terry, getting up. "I must go and sort things out finally. Don, will you take my car and drive the twins home? There's a police car out-side for me."

" Of course," said Don. "When would you like your car back, if ever?"

"To-night and in one piece," said Terry, firmly. "Pick me up about eight o'clock, will you? I should be nearly through by then."

"Right," agreed Don. "Come on, twins."

"Good-bye," said Julie. " And thank you very much. I know we were very tiresome and difficult at first, and it was nice of you to—to——"

"Put up with us," finished June. "I hope we'll see you again some day soon."

"That's all right. I hope so, too. Good-bye," said Terry, and waved to them as they climbed into the little red Bug with Don.

"It's certainly been fun," said June, as Don drove away with them.

" And that reminds me, I completely forgot to ask Terry about the open envelope at the library," exclaimed Julie. "I wonder if he found out who had opened it."

"Yes, he told me," said Don. "It was a youngster who was watching—he saw us all go shooting out after Mr. Carruthers, and apparently he saw the envelope on the floor. He picked it up, opened it, and, having failed to make head or tail of it, he simply pushed it back into the book, dusted his fingertips and walked quietly away."

"Good gracious, how on earth did Terry find all that out?"

"They have their methods," said Don, mysteriously.

"And I was so hoping it would be a crook with a gang of—a gang of gangsters and guns and all that sort of thing," said June sadly.

"You blood-thirsty creatures," said Don. "However, if that's your taste, we'll do our best to oblige next time."

The twins laughed.

"I'd love there to be a next time," said Julie.

"Me too," agreed June.

Don drew up outside their house, got out and, with his hand on his heart, bowed elegantly.

"We'll do our best," he promised.

"Won't you come in?" asked Julie.

"And face your bloodhounds?" asked Don. "Not likely. I've always been allergic to sausages since the day when my elder brother——"

In the distance, Sausage and Mash could be heard barking shrilly, as they raced across the garden to greet the twins.

"I'll tell you another time," said Don, leaping into the car.

"We'll hold you to it," called Julie. "Don't forget."

Don waved a hand.

"It's a promise. I'll save it for the next adventure," he called as he drove off.

"It's a date," cried the twins.

In silence, they watched the small red car go skittering down the road until it vanished round a distant corner.

Then, with the two excited Dachshunds jumping round them, they strolled together across the garden into the house, fingering the rosemary pendants as they went.

The End